Summer Dreaming

Little Hondo Press

Contact: littlehondopress@yahoo.com

Summer Dreaming – Hot in the Hamptons

Copyright © 2015 Elizabeth Matis

Digital ISBN: 978-0-9908848-2-2

Print ISBN: 978-0-9908848-3-5

Cover Design by: Billington Media

Print Edition

This is a work of fiction. Names, characters, places and incidents either are products of the author's imagination or are used fictitiously. Any resemblance to actual events or locales or persons, living or dead, is entirely coincidental.

Also by Liz Matis

Summer Dreaming
Hot in the Hampton Series

I'm looking for a hero. Not.

You'd think as a new college grad I'd be looking for the perfect job and the perfect man. Well, I'm not. Summer is here and instead of plotting my future, I'm playing in the Hamptons with my two best friends. Sun and sex is all I'm looking for. Then I meet Sean Dempsey, my fantasy lifeguard in the flesh. But he is more than just a hot bod with a whistle. Much more. And after he makes a daring save, I'm thinking a hero is exactly what I've been looking for all along.

To the rescue…

By day I guard the beaches in the Hamptons, by night I've had my fair share of summer flings. Then I meet Kelsey Mitchell, a girl with eyes like the setting sun and I burn for more. Much more. Something I have no right to ask of her…forever.

Love burns hotter in the Hamptons. Come play.

Dear Reader,

Come play in the Hamptons sandbox with the Hot In the Hamptons series, a trilogy featuring SUMMER DREAMING (Liz Matis), SUMMER TEMPTATION (Wendy S. Marcus), and SUMMER SINS (Jennifer Probst). Three separate novellas. Three different authors. One summer to remember.

Read them all, or just read one. It's up to you! But when read together you'll find extra story scenes to enhance your reading pleasure. No matter which route you choose, these standalone novellas will make you burn.

Thank you to awesome authors Jennifer Probst and Wendy S. Marcus for taking on the Hot in the Hamptons series with me. You guys rock!

Summer Dreaming

The Hot in the Hamptons Series

by Liz Matis

Prologue

I HALF LISTENED to the valedictorian speech. But the cliché phrases 'Seize the day' and 'Seize every opportunity' caught my attention.

If only it were that easy. Unlike my friends who had big career plans, I remained undecided of a path. But I didn't have to worry about that today or for the whole summer. After the ceremony I was flying home to Georgia to help with my sister's prom and high school graduation, then I was free to drive to the Hamptons in New York to spend the summer with my two best friends. One last hurrah to be young and carefree, before the adult world crashed the party.

Before Storme married her supposed Prince Charming. Not that Philip was a bad guy, but he was the wrong guy for her. Just like her business degree was wrong for her. Not that I ever said anything about either her choice in men or career. I smiled over at my friend as she tucked a stray hair under her cap.

Though she tried to tame the black wild curls, she was fighting a losing battle with the heat. Meanwhile, me, with straight blonde hair would kill for a little volume.

And at summer's end, brainiac and summa cum laude, Leigh was off to a high-powered public relations job in New York City. Only right now she looked as pale as her father who'd recently had a heart attack. Maybe she was hung over? Come to think of it, she hadn't touched her drink last night. Leigh looked anxiously at her father in the stands. She'd been so stressed out between his illness and finals, no wonder she looked as if she were about to keel over. That had to be it, nothing a little sun and fun wouldn't cure!

"Kelsey Mitchell, degree in Architectural Engineering and minor in Art."

From the stands, my mom and two sisters cheered like I'd just scored a point on the Volleyball court, but there was one voice painfully absent—my father's. I accepted my degree with unshed tears realizing this would only be the first of many milestones my dad would miss.

Chapter 1

Sean

FROM MY SPOT in the parking lot, I whistled at the rare beauty. Sleek and sexy, the sunlight shone off her curves. She hummed like a dream. Man, I wanted to take her for a long, fast ride.

Then like something out of a wet dream, *she* slid out of the dark blue 1968 Mustang Shelby GT.

I was a breast man, pure and simple. As a lifeguard for six years, I'd seen plenty. From small and perky to large and full, I didn't discriminate. I loved the feel of the soft flesh in my hands and the way they felt pressed against my chest during sex. Loved the gentle moan of a woman responding to my mouth sucking on her nipple.

The blonde, though, had her breasts hiding behind a gold t-shirt. In white lettering the word 'Angel' stretched across the front. For my sake, I hoped that wasn't true.

Because the white micro-mini skirt she wore left her long, shapely legs bare. An image of those legs wrapped around me, pulling me in deeper, revved my engines.

A woman who could handle the piece of American muscle she drove could definitely handle mine.

Man, I wanted to take the blonde for a long, slow ride.

I had to meet the owner of the hot rod and of that smoking bod, but I had no business pursuing a relationship. With the promise to my parents to wait four years fulfilled, at this summer's end I'd be sweating it out in basic training, then heading off to God only knew. Luckily most rich girls didn't seem to have a problem with a summer fling with a local who wasn't husband material. I'd learned that the hard way. Twice. With a car worth about a hundred grand, she had to be loaded. She'd break my heart without a thought. *Three times a charm.*

Unable to stop myself, I jumped out of my Jeep and followed her into the drugstore. Spotting the flowing mane of hair, I covertly entered the next aisle over and pretended to shop. I'd been with plenty of blondes, but she didn't seem like the typical stuck up, wealthy Hampton summer resident. I liked that she wasn't overly made up like all the girls who descended on my hometown each summer. I doubted she thought about makeup before hitting the beach. She was…what was the word? Breezy. Natural. Mine.

She looked up, our gazes meeting over the shelving that separated the aisle. Despite being caught staring, I couldn't look away. The light brown eyes peeking back at me reminded me of the sun setting over the ocean after a sweltering day.

"Hi, ya."

Her sweet Southern accent spoke directly to my cock. My body heated like a third-degree sunburn.

Before I could respond with even a grunt, she turned and approached the cash register. I followed, but realizing I had nothing to buy, I grabbed an item off the end cap shelving and slid in line behind her. *Nice ass, too.*

She turned and arched an eyebrow, catching my gaze. "Checking out my assets?"

I laughed. Funny, too. I was in trouble. My cock hardened. Big, big trouble.

"Guilty, as charged." I noticed what she was holding. Tampons. "Bummer." *Crap.* I didn't mean to say that out loud.

"You have no idea." She laughed and tossed the box onto the counter. Nodding to the package in my hand, she said, "Or maybe you do, huh?"

I looked down, horrified to find a package of sanitary pads.

Why couldn't it be a box of extra large condoms?

She charmed the cashier with politeness. Or it might have been the accent, but the words 'please' and 'thank you' flowed naturally from her mouth. Yes, she definitely wasn't the typical Hampton summer resident, except she didn't spare me another glance as she left the store.

I tossed the offending package I held into a bin by the door and followed her yet again. Was I crossing the line into stalker territory? "Wait up," I shouted.

But she was already waiting outside the door with a big smile. "Did you forget something?" She nodded to my empty hands.

Relieved that she hadn't run off, I slowed and we naturally fell into step as we walked to her car.

"The truth is, I'd just gotten back to my Jeep when you pulled in. I had to meet you."

"Had to?"

Had to. Wanted to. Needed to. Same difference. "Are you here for the summer?"

"Yes, and you?"

"I lifeguard over at Main Beach." We reached her car door. I stuck out a hand. "Sean Dempsey."

A graceful hand stretched out. I noted the lack of nail polish as her long fingers slid into my palm. There was no cliché electric shock when we touched but my cock ached, already anticipating her silky grip around my thick base. *Down boy.*

"I'm Kelsey."

No last name. Smart girl.

"Nice car."

The light in her eyes dulled. What did I say? Did she think I was only after her for a chance to drive her car? For the first time in my life it seemed like I'd blown a pickup but that didn't bother me as much as the sadness in her eyes did.

After a moment she said, "It belonged to my Dad."

Belonged? Past tense. "I'm sorry."

Uh-oh. Tears. I should run while I had the chance but I stood rooted to my spot, fascinated by the way her eyes seemed to swim in sunshine. Fascinated by her.

Chapter 2

Kelsey

I BIT MY lip to keep the tears at bay. Just what a cute guy wanted, a girl with her period and on the edge of hysterics. Only the tampons weren't for me.

I peeked up, his once flirty blue eyes now filled with concern. He looked sincerely sorry. And not the 'Shit, I'm not getting laid tonight' type of sorry. There was no way for Sean to know that while the car was a beautiful memory of my father's love, it was also a constant reminder that my Dad was gone. My heart tightened in grief.

What did one say to 'I'm sorry' regarding the death of a loved one? Even after one year, I couldn't figure that out. It wasn't like it was Sean's fault. I said a lame, "Thank you."

The standard awkward silence I knew to expect followed. Actually, I found any silence unsettling. It made me say stupid thinks like, "Is that a torpedo buoy in your shorts or are you just happy to see me". My lame attempt at lifeguard humor was thankfully thwarted as a blaring horn broke the morning quiet. I looked to the road to see a bunch of girls, obviously beach bound, waving out the car windows. "Hey, Sean."

With his gorgeous face and a lean but muscular body, I wasn't surprised to witness his popularity with the ladies, but he didn't turn his head to the road, instead he kept his gaze on me. Interesting.

But was he going to ask me out or not? I may be a feminist but as a Southern lady—snort—it was bred into me that a gentlemen asked for the first date, paid for the first date, and initiated the first kiss. Not that there were many gentlemen left in the world. And I wasn't always the perfect Southern lady. Most of the time, I was. Sometimes. When it suited me.

"Well, it was nice to meet you, Sean," I blurted and swung the car door open.

"Wait." He touched my arm and then backed away, dragging a hand through his wavy black hair. "Can I get your number?"

Besides playing it safe, I believed in having the ball in my court, so I said. "No, but you can give me yours." I offered a smile to soften the blow of my refusal.

His face registered shock. He probably never had to work at getting a girl before. As a lifeguard, he'd just twirl his whistle, flex his bicep, flash that bad boy smile and the beach bunnies would simply drop their bikini bottoms. How many girls had feigned drowning to get those lips of his on hers?

I never gave much thought to that part of a man's anatomy, but Sean's promised soft kisses. Now I bit my lip for an entirely different reason.

Sean shot off his number and I entered it into my phone. "Got it." I waved the phone in the air and slid into the car. He shut the door, leaned his corded forearms on the frame of the open window, and dipped his head. "You're not playing me?"

I swallowed hard, gripping the steering wheel to keep from pulling that beautiful boy into my car for a make-out session right in the middle of the drugstore parking lot.

"I don't play games." I was just being safe the way my dad had taught me to be and besides I liked to take the lead with men. It threw them off balance. As soon as I got to Storme's house, I'd Google Sean Dempsey, before checking out the popular social media sites to make sure he wasn't a serial dater or a psychopath.

My best friend spent every summer in the Hamptons, maybe she knew him.

"Cool, talk to you soon, Kelsey." He smiled, winked, and then tapped the top of the car twice before turning towards his Jeep.

The orange board shorts he wore hugged his cute ass. The white t-shirt clung to his lean muscled body. The words Ocean Rescue stretched across his broad shoulders. I started the engine. The soft rumble of the seats only added to the throbbing between my legs.

Sean had already won the starring role in my lifeguard fantasy. And I hadn't even touched a grain of sand yet.

I DROVE UP to Storme's sprawling family estate. My mouth dropped, marveling at the size. "Stay out at our summer cottage in the Hamptons," she had said. The shingled summer cottage was a mansion by any standards. I knew her family had money, but holy crap, I never knew she was billionaire rich.

I turned off the car and ran a hand along the dashboard. At least the Shelby Mustang looked like it belonged here. Me, in my thrift store chic clothes, didn't. I glanced in the rearview mirror at the flea market sunglasses I wore.

My friends had never made me feel like I didn't belong. Still, I rarely went shopping with them. In school, I either had a nonexistent paper to write or fake practice to attend. Not that my family was poor. But even with the volleyball scholarship, I wouldn't have been able to attend Penn State if it wasn't for the scholarship fund the Atlanta Storm baseball team had set up for the sons and daughters of soldiers killed in action.

Upon my graduation from college, the car my father had lovingly restored over a decade had become mine. Not only had my mother given the okay for me to sell it, she'd encouraged me to accept one of the multiple offers I'd already received on it. But I couldn't bring myself to part with the only physical reminder of my Dad. Even if selling the Mustang would provide me with enough money for my graduate studies overseas.

During the school year, I'd earned enough by waitressing to pay for the insurance this summer. After that, I'd have to take it off the road until I had a steady job in…well, that was the problem wasn't it?

But for now, the whole summer stretched out before me. Parties. Beach. Sun. And lifeguards. Sean.

Remembering the paper bag, I grabbed it before stepping out of the car. I breathed in the salted air. Already feeling lighter, I pulled one of my suitcases from the trunk and headed for the house.

Storme greeted me at the door, wrapping me in a hug like it was our ten-year reunion instead of six weeks since graduation.

Backing away, I tossed the paper bag to Storme. I wondered if Sean would have believed me if I'd told him they were for a friend.

"How much do I owe you?" she asked, heading for her purse on the counter.

I followed, taking in the impeccable white walls and dark floors. If it weren't for the pop of color from the pillows, the place would've looked sterile. I was about to make a joke about the tampons costing a hundred dollars, but sometimes Storme was more self-conscious about being rich than I was about being…well…not rich.

"Seriously? It's a box of tampons. Besides, if it weren't for your period, I wouldn't have met the hottest guy ever to walk the planet."

Storme's eyes widened. "Already? You haven't

even unpacked your bags yet!"

With a dramatic hair flip, I said, "It's the boobs. Men are defenseless against them."

"And your sweet southern accent that makes cursing sound like a compliment," added Storme.

"It's an art," I admitted. "When is Leigh arriving?"

"Later today. She tried to back out, but I laid the biggest guilt trip on her. An art I learned from my mother."

And as a victim of, I thought, otherwise Storme would have been a graduate of the Fashion Institute instead of Penn State, her mother's Alma Mater.

Storme hooked me by the arm. "I'll show you to your room and then let your summer of debauchery commence!"

We started up the grand staircase. I felt like I had walked onto the set of the TV show *Revenge*. I worried again about my wardrobe. This home lent itself to elegant women wearing high fashion, not college girls who planned to live in bikinis all summer. My teeth tugged on my lip remembering we weren't college girls any longer.

"So tell me more about this hot guy."

"He's a lifeguard."

"You don't mess around, do you?" she said regarding my mission to land a lifeguard this summer. "Is he cute?"

"You have no idea. Six-two, black wavy hair, blue eyes that invite you to dive in and drown."

Storme halted mid-step and I nearly ran into her. She whirled around and grabbed my arm. "Sean Dempsey?"

"You know him?" By the widening of my friend's eyes, she did. "Should I be jealous?"

"No! I'm getting married, remember?" Storme released her grip and put her hands on her hips. "It's just that at the pool party tonight I'd planned to introduce you to one of Philip's golf buddies. But leave it to Kelsey Mitchell to come to the Hamptons, a hotbed of fabulously rich men, and hook up with the poorest boy around."

"Dollar signs don't mean a thing between the sheets." It wouldn't matter if Sean didn't have a dime. Money had never impressed me. Reaching the landing, I fished for more information. "What else can you tell me about Sean?"

"The summer girls call him 'The Hampton Hottie'."

Before I could ask Storme to expand, she opened

the door and said, "Here you go. I hope you like it."

Unlike the downstairs decor, the room was decorated in a casual beach theme. Still, it looked like a page out of a magazine. The crisp white comforter on the queen-sized bed invited me for a nap. Fueled on Red Bull and on the excitement to reach the Hamptons, the long drive from Georgia settled in my bones.

"The bathroom is through that door," said Storme.

"I have my own bathroom?" I risked looking uncool and rushed in. The decor mirrored the bedroom. Seashells and candles lined the lip of a jetted tub, a steam shower with several shower sprays beckoned, and a marble vanity with a place to sit and put on makeup. If I were the squealing type, I'd be squealing like an annoying fourteen-year-old girl.

Growing up, I'd shared a bathroom with two sisters and then at college with my sorority ones.

From the door Storme said, "I'll let you settle in. Come down when you're ready and we'll have something to eat. Then we'll drink Chardonnay on the deck while we watch the sunset in style until Leigh arrives." Storme went to leave but peeked back in. "Sorry, no lifeguards by my stretch of the beach."

Beachfront house, check. Money, check. Chardonnay, check. No lifeguards? Guess it's true you can't have it all.

Chapter 3

Sean

I HUNG BY the pool as the partygoers tried to drowned themselves in alcohol. Stone cold sober, I kept watch over the illuminated water, ignoring the chaos around me. After rescuing people from the ocean, saving someone from a pool was easy money. If the rich parents of a twenty-two-year-old entitled punk, who'd never worked a day in his life, wanted to pay me a hundred bucks an hour to lifeguard at their home to prevent a lawsuit, who was I to complain?

Why someone would go to the expense of building a pool when the Atlantic Ocean was in your backyard, I couldn't understand. That was rich people for you. Materialistic assholes. With a red plastic cup filled with ice next to me, and a phone to my ear, I tried to blend in as requested.

The money I earned during my summers had

bankrolled my trips around the world during the off-season. But at the end of this one, I'd be headed out for a different kind of adventure.

I wasn't going to work parties since I wanted to enjoy the summer nights before I headed to boot camp, but my buddy had a hot date and had pleaded with me to take his spot. I was all about helping a bro out, especially when I had nothing going on tonight. Hot Rod Chick hadn't called and I wasn't going to hold my breath. So what if every time my phone rang I looked at the screen hoping for an 'unknown number' to pop up.

I told myself, it's for the best. One taste of Kelsey and I'd need another and then another. I knew this because I was full of shit. I'd been smiling like an idiot all day just thinking about her. It bothered me that she hadn't called even if it had only been twelve hours since she'd typed my number into her phone.

"It's for the best," I repeated to myself. Summer romances never lasted. And that's all it could ever be. Once I entered boot camp, my life wouldn't be my own.

I had always dreamed of serving my country. I had been anxious to see the summer fly by, that was until I'd met Kelsey. The prospect of spending the summer in her arms made me want to slow down time. But she hadn't called.

Lifeguarding had always been more than a seasonal job. I loved the lifestyle, and I admit, I loved the rush that came with rescuing a life, but it wasn't a career path unless I moved to a place like California. College had never been on my radar. Not that I was stupid, far from it, but I was what you'd call a 'hands on' type of guy.

Too bad I'd never get them on that Hot Rod Chick's smoking body.

Over the blaring hip-hop music, I heard a lounge chair scratching along the brick patio. I ignored it. I was responsible for the pool and nothing else.

"No!" A loud female voice with a Southern accent had my head snapping up.

Kelsey.

Kelsey, who hadn't called.

Kelsey, who was letting a trust fund pussy, paw at her body.

No, not letting. She pushed away from him and made eye contact with me.

Her pretty mouth worded, "Save me."

Well, in or out of the water, I was lifeguard first.

To prevent a scene, I quickly decided to play the

boyfriend angle. Yeah, right. I wanted to claim that girl as mine and make sure the only hands exploring those curves were my own. "Kelsey, babe. I've been looking for you."

"Sean!"

Saying my name in her now sweet drawl drove me wild. What would she sound like when I made her come?

"You didn't say you had a boyfriend," said the trust fund pussy.

"She shouldn't have to. No, means, no," I said.

"Sometimes, it means maybe."

"*Maybe*, this will make it more clear." Kelsey stomped on the guy's bare foot with the spiked heel of her shoe. The ruffles at the bottom of her yellow mini dress flounced showing off more leg than I supposed she intended. I itched to play with the fabric and find out what lay beneath.

"Bitch."

I wasn't the jealous type, so when a wave of possessiveness flooded my body, it took me by surprise. My hand curled into a fist, but Kelsey's fingers caressed mine, easing the rage to a ripple.

"Creeper," said Kelsey.

With a slight limp, the trust fund pussy skulked

off into the throng of partiers.

"Thank you for coming to my rescue."

If that little show was anything to go by, then she hadn't needed my help at all.

The scent of vanilla wafted in the air, tempting me to nuzzle the delicate curve of her neck. I leaned forward and whispered, "Too bad you didn't require mouth-to-mouth. It's one my specialties." I pulled back so I could see her reaction.

Her eyes widened. "Oh, lifeguard humor."

I lifted her hand, brushing a kiss on her wrist. "It's no joke."

She tugged on her bottom lip in that cute way of hers. Damn, I wanted to do the job myself. Tug, lick, kiss, and more. Much more.

A splash sounded. I tore my gaze away from her hot mouth and scanned the pool. I had broken a cardinal rule of lifeguarding. Never look away from the water. Easy going as I was, I took my duties as a lifeguard seriously.

Luckily, the guys performing cannonballs weren't drowning. Horseplay was fine by me, but when combined with alcohol it made for a dangerous mix. I couldn't yell 'no jumping' without embarrassing the host of the party. This wasn't the local pool with a gang of preadolescent boys being boys. This was worse. Prevention was half the battle of lifeguarding. In this situation, I was unable to stop the inevitable. I was on standby until someone hurt themselves.

I turned back to Kelsey. "Sorry, I'm on duty." With my eyes back on the water, I continued, "I moonlight as a private lifeguard."

"I didn't know there was such a thing."

"Go figure."

"No red shorts?"

I wore blue ones. "Not tonight."

"Not even a whistle?"

"Yeah, that would make me real popular at a party like this. I'm supposed to fit in."

"Well, you're doing a terrible job."

"How so?"

"You're not stupid ass drunk."

I laughed. "I do have that going for me." I didn't dare turn my head, not even for a quick glance. If I did, I might not be able to peel my gaze away from how the light of the pool made her eyes seem like liquid fire. And that mouth! I wondered what she tasted like. Vanilla?

"Who are you here with?"

"Two of my girlfriends. Speaking of which, I

should go find them."

I wondered if I knew them. "I'll be here until 1:00 AM if you need me."

"Good to know."

I risked that glance. Her smile promised her return.

But she didn't. Either some slick playboy got to her or Kelsey was playing hard to get. Hard to get I could work with. I could play that game with the best of them.

Chapter 4

Kelsey

MY EYES OPENED to the sun streaming through the window. Making a mental note to draw the shades tonight, I rolled over and pulled the covers over my head. My muscles ached from the long drive, a day at the beach, and then partying all night. I felt guilty for abandoning Sean, but he was on the job and I wanted his full attention. There'd be plenty of time this summer to explore the depths of his blue-eyed gaze, unless he had found someone else last night. I whipped off the covers. Maybe it was time to call him. Reaching for my cell phone on the nightstand, I groaned at the time. 7:00 AM. I guessed it was a little early so I flopped to my back for a long, lazy stretch. A girl could get used to this life.

A long run on the beach would get my blood pumping. Ever since the volleyball season ended, I'd been running to keep in shape. Maybe there was a 5k I could enter to satisfy my need for competition. Growing up a tomboy, it was never about how could I look pretty, but how I could I win.

I hadn't even worn makeup until my senior year in high school when my younger sister had held an intervention of sorts. It was embarrassing.

I slid out of bed before the comfortable mattress lulled me back to sleep. I knew better than to attempt to wake up Storme or Leigh this early, never mind ask them to go for a run. I was on my own, which was okay with me.

Dressed in peach-colored shorts and a t-shirt, I hit the sand running. Thoughts raced around my mind faster than my feet were carrying my body. When the summer was over, so was playtime in the Hamptons sandbox. Was it time to grow up and get a job or follow my heart and further my studies in architecture in Europe? Or something else entirely? After four years of college I should have had it all figured out, but I was just as confused as ever. I wondered what advice my Dad would've given me and if I would've listened. It's not like I ever listened to my mother's. What daughter does?

I don't know if it was the salted air or the sound

of waves but I hit that zone, and all my worries flew away on the ocean breeze. Or maybe, I was simply in denial.

Not used to running on the wet sand, my legs began to burn and I slowed up. My Fitbit read 3 miles. I hadn't planned on going so far. I was about to turn around for a nice easy stroll back to the house when farther down the beach I spotted a group of shirtless guys in red shorts. Lifeguards? Sean?

I found some extra fuel in my tank and casually jogged over. As I approached, I angled off to the dry sand and sat at a discreet distance, yet still close enough to ogle Sean and the other lifeguards performing sprints, pushups, and jumping jacks.

Too bad there wasn't some male revue music to go along with my private show.

The guys were all in great shape, but Sean stood out. It was more than the tattoo of an eagle inked across his back or his shorts riding a little lower on his hips giving me a glimpse of oblique's that my hands itched to claw at. Okay, it was a lot of that, but he also wore a look of determination like he was training for something more.

"Want to volunteer as our practice victim?" A cute guy with surfer-long blonde hair called up to me.

Did I ever!

"Sure." I sprang up to dust the sand off my bottom then I walked to the group of guys and five women. Did I forget to mention them?

"It's too cold for her," claimed Sean.

Was he trying to ruin my fun? Was he jealous? "I can handle a little cold water."

"You don't have a bathing suit on," said Sean.

"Yes, I do." To prove my point I stripped off my shirt, baring a lime green bikini bra top that held my girls in place. I could give Kate Upton's boobs a run for their money. The whistles I heard proved it but my eyes were all for Sean, who did not drop his gaze to my rack.

Keeping eye contact with me, he said, "Sorry, Blake. This one is mine."

Did Sean mean as a practice victim or as his girl? I shimmied out of my shorts to reveal a matching bikini bottom.

"I'm the one who asked," said Blake.

"Too bad." Sean touched my arm, leading me down to the water's edge. "You can swim, right?"

"Like a mermaid," I said in a flirty tone, drawling out my accent. I wasn't about to say like a fish because even though fish symbolized concepts like fertility, they were not sexy.

"You got a great set of seashells."

His smile made me feel reckless. "Aren't mermaids topless?" I feigned reaching for the hooks of my bikini top.

"Let's not start a riot." Sean thumbed to the group of lifeguards watching on as if we were the entertainment for the day.

I looked out to the ocean. "What do I do?"

"Swim out past the breakers."

"And then what?"

"Then let me do what I do second best."

Second best? The freezing water shocked my body numb, but cooled my heated thoughts of Sean's first best. I stumbled as a wave crashed into my midsection. Navigating the Atlantic Ocean took some getting used to. Growing up near the Gulf of Mexico, I was used to warmer waters and calmer seas.

I heard a whistle. "That's far enough," called Sean.

I turned to face the shore and embraced the part of drowning woman. "Help! Help! Oh save me!" *And hurry because I'm freezing.*

Sean's shark-like smile before he dove into the surf had me gulping like I'd taken in a wave full of seawater. I struggled for a breath, feeling like I was drowning for real. Maybe, I was.

Chapter 5

Sean

BLAKE WAS A dead man for asking Kelsey to play the victim, but I couldn't blame him for trying. Any lifeguard would consider her the catch of the season, never mind the catch of the day. Luckily, I'd already hooked Kelsey. I just had to play it cool to reel her in.

Normally, the lifeguards practiced on each other so I wasn't used to practicing on a hot babe. I reminded myself to act like a professional. I preached the safety rules and regulations like it was the Ten Commandments. I had to set a good example, especially for the younger lifeguards.

With each stroke I prepared myself for the save, even if it was a mock one. Each rescue involved a series of decisions. In rough water, Blake and I would have tag-teamed it, one swimming out with a torpedo buoy and the other using the line to pull the victim back to shore. If a swimmer was farther out, we'd use surfboards. But since practice rescues weren't on the morning workout schedule I had none of that.

ON A PERFECT white flag day, like today, I was doing it old school. There was no need for Blake or any of the other guards to get involved.

Surfacing, I swept the water, even though like a dolphin's radar I knew exactly where Kelsey was. With ten more feet to go, I ducked my head in the water.

As I zeroed in, I fought the urge to take her into my arms and kiss her.

It didn't matter that'd I'd seen hundreds of hot babes on the beach before. Kelsey was… different. I couldn't explain it. Not yet.

I surfaced in front of her. "I'm here to save the day."

"Gee, I was hoping for that Hoff guy."

"This ain't *Baywatch*, babe."

My training kicked in. I grabbed her right arm with my right hand, and in one motion pulled her to me as I turned her around. Ignoring the tinge of pink on her shoulders, I hooked my arms underneath her into the cross-chest carry and began to kick.

I was the fucking poster boy for lifeguarding. Until she moved. With my body beneath hers, her ass bumped my dick, sparking an arousal I wasn't prepared for.

"Don't help," I said more sternly than I should have, but I was frustrated. All eyes were on us. This wasn't the time or place to play ocean games even if the siren in my arms tempted me from my post.

"Sorry."

Now I felt bad. If a victim was able, they could help kick to shore, but the thought of Kelsey, accidentally or purposely rubbing up against me, and I'd be the one in need of rescue.

I needed a distraction from the way her long hair floated in the water, exactly like the mermaid she'd claimed to be.

"So do you come to this beach often?"

"Oh, more lifeguard humor. Do you talk to all your victims this way?"

"I make conversation to reassure them." Which was true, but I'd never used a lame line like that before.

Our limbs tangled as I let a gentle wave carry us the rest of the way to shore. I dragged her arm around my shoulder like she was any other drowning victim and helped her to her feet.

Blake jogged down to help.

"I got it," I said and he wisely backed away.

Circling my arm around her waist, we stumbled to the dry sand. Without the water to cool me, my body heated and I was surprised not to see steam rising off me. I eased her to the sand and handed her my towel.

She blotted her face and I noticed a sprinkle of freckles across the bridge of her nose. I hadn't seen them yesterday. With her hair slicked back, her eyes seemed like twin setting suns. Being in her orbit made me feel dizzy, like I'd been out in the heat all day.

Still, I wanted to lick each salty droplet off of Kelsey's skin.

She patted the towel just above the swell of her breasts. "What about your specialty?"

I smiled. There was nothing I'd liked better than to give Kelsey mouth-to-mouth. But I couldn't trust her not to turn it into a kiss. Hell, I couldn't trust myself. Not even with my co-workers watching on.

"With you chatting during the rescue I figured you didn't need it."

"Me?" She tossed a handful of sand at my feet.

"You're the one who wouldn't shut up."

True, I hadn't. Talking kept me from thinking about how her body floated against mine. Kelsey's soft, lush curves and me, totally the opposite.

"Well, thank you for saving me."

"Anytime."

She batted her eyelashes. "How will I ever repay you?" The drawl sweetened and thickened, like honey.

Man, I could think of a few things. A lot of things. "A date. Dinner."

"Seeing how you just saved my life, I don't know how I could refuse."

I never expected anything from a rescue, not that I'd really saved her, but I liked where this game was leading. "Then don't."

"Tell me when and where to meet you."

What was up with the cloak and dagger antics? Was she playing it safe? Or was she afraid her mother or friends would disapprove of her going out with a townie? It wouldn't be the first time. What did I care, as long as I got to taste Kelsey's skin? "Tonight, at seven. The Bar at Surf's Lodge in Montauk."

"See you then." Kelsey leapt up.

"Can I get your last name?"

"No." She tossed back my towel. Each time I used it that day I'd torture myself with the picture of her drying off her beautiful body. But my torment intensified the second she bent over to pick up her clothes. There were more freckles leading up her calves and thighs to the edge of her bikini bottom. I itched to play a game of connect the dots along her skin, first with my fingers and then with my tongue. Her perfect heart shaped ass begged for my hand to spank it.

Kelsey turned and smiled like she knew exactly what I was thinking. "Oh and next time, I expect the full lifeguard experience."

"Yes, ma'am."

The long legs that had been entangled with mine now took her away from me. Tonight, I hoped they'd be wrapped around me, pulling me into her. Revealing her secrets.

"Ah, my mysterious Kelsey, maybe you are a mermaid after all," I said to the wind. A long day on the lifeguard stand stretched out before me. Tonight couldn't come fast enough.

Blake came up from behind and slapped my shoulder. "Bro, I'd like to obstruct that babe's airway."

My blood boiled at the thought of my friend anywhere near Kelsey. She was mine. I wanted to thump my chest and yell it to the world. Instead, I kept it light. "Sorry, Bro, the only whistle she'll be blowing this summer is mine."

"Lucky bastard."

I certainly was. We bumped fists and got back to business.

Chapter 6
Kelsey

WHY WAS I so nervous? Sean was just another a guy, I told myself for the thousandth time. So, yeah he was drop panty gorgeous, but I wasn't wearing any. Performing a twirl in front of the mirror, the turquoise sundress, which hit just above my knees, did not reveal my secret. I sat at the vanity like a girly girl but I applied my makeup with a light touch. Some BB cream to hide my freckles, a stroke of waterproof mascara on each blondish eyelash, and a swipe of pink gloss across my lips completed a casual look for a casual date. Only my feelings didn't feel casual when it came to Sean.

I looked up the directions to The Surf Lodge on my phone. Thirty minutes by car? Why so far from the hotbed of restaurants and bars in town? Was he afraid of running into his harem? A girlfriend? Upon further interrogation, Storme revealed that she had remembered him from a couple of bonfire parties a few years back and she warned me that he had always been with a different girl. Was he still the same way now?

Not that I cared but since I had ten minutes to spare before I had to leave, I decided to do a little cyber snooping on my date. Sean's Instagram account revealed nothing shocking, and his privacy settings on his Facebook account prevented me from seeing any details. Going back to the search page, I scrolled down and found an article from last year detailing his rescue of a celebrity who had thought the posted red flags didn't apply to him. Sean was declared a hero, but he probably made rescues like that all the time and this save had only made the paper because the victim had been famous.

The ten minutes passed quickly so I breezed out the door before my friends had a chance to ambush me with questions. Or before they could yell at me to wear panties.

As I drove my father's car to my date, I wondered what my dad would have thought of Sean. Great Kelsey, just what you want Sean to see.

Tears and runny mascara.

Cranking the radio to Train's song about mermaids, I sung along with abandon trying to drown out the thoughts of my dad. Driving into the parking lot of The Surf Lodge, I admired the large white clapboard house. It looked like the perfect beach getaway. I pulled up next to Sean's beat up Jeep, wondering if he ever rode it on the beach.

I grabbed my crochet purse, the contents included a condom neatly tucked away in the zipper compartment. Before I could open the door, Sean did and held out his hand. I was blown away by this gesture as I slipped my hand into his. Despite being in his arms earlier during the rescue, this simple contact sent a delicious hum through my body. I smoothed out my dress as Sean's gaze swept my body from toe to head.

Reaching my eyes he said, "You're beautiful."

I tugged at my bottom lip as I did a survey of my own. His large feet were in sandals, his pressed khaki shorts fell just above the knee and a gauzy white shirt had two buttons undone. A brown leather necklace completed his GQ beach look. His black hair was freshly washed but unruly curls escaped the gel he must have applied. He looked manly and boyish all at the same time, making me a jumble of schoolgirl nervous and womanly want. Maybe I should have worn panties.

"Come on, you look hungry," Sean said. His predator smile and heated blue eyes revealed his own starvation for me.

We walked into the lobby and I immediately loved the cool vibe. There was a horseshoe shaped lounge area and behind it a huge piece of driftwood with lit candles perched on top. My artist's eye appreciated the vivid photography on the wall. It was the perfect mix of clean lines and boho chic. Entering the bar area, my gaze was drawn to the ceiling of wood rafters with colorful surfboards lying haphazardly on top of the beams. The chair-like bar stools matched the color of my dress. As much as I loved the inside, we were led outside.

Long picnic tables stretched out under a slew of wire baskets. Each one had a light bulb. Dusk was just beginning to settle around us. Additional strings of tiny lights were lit in the lounge area beyond the dining area. A fire pit waited on the sand. It was almost magical. Or maybe it was the boy I was with.

"Is this okay?"

"More than okay. Is the food as good as the atmosphere?"

Sean nodded.

I took a peek at the menu, relieved to find the prices reasonable. I knew lifeguards didn't make much money and I'd feel really bad if Sean blew his paycheck on me. The value of a dollar had been instilled in me at an early age.

Beer is normally my drink of choice but the Endless Summer cocktail, with vodka, chardonnay, lemon, and muddled red grapes sounded too refreshing to pass up.

The cute waitress took my drink order with a sneer but bestowed a wide smile and a wink for Sean when she asked what he wanted. I wondered if I should be worried about her poisoning my food.

My drink arrived in a mason jar. I hesitated for a second, but the straw beckoned me to sip. "Ah, heaven."

Looking at my lips Sean said, "It sure is." Then he took a long pull of his beer.

The waitress cleared her throat.

I ordered the lobster roll and chips and Sean ordered oysters. Hmmm… I wondered if oysters really did have aphrodisiac powers. Not that Sean looked like he needed any help. He radiated strength and virility.

"Do you surf?" I asked.

"Yep. You?"

"Not a lot of good breaks in Georgia."

He leaned forward. "I was wondering where that accent came from."

"I don't have an accent. Y'all have the accent," I teased.

"You're the foreigner here. I'm just a townie."

"I don't think you're just anything, Sean Dempsey." I slipped my foot from my sandal and grazed my toes upward along his calf.

"Damn girl." He swatted my foot away. "Don't start something you can't finish, you won't like the consequences." He took another long pull of beer like he was trying to satisfy his thirst for me.

"Maybe, I would."

Sean nearly spat out his beer. He recovered, swallowing the beer with a gulp.

I laughed, loving how I made this All-American male stumble. He was the one who was used to making girls blush and act like fawning idiots.

"I've never met anyone like you."

Despite knowing it had to be a line from his arsenal, I felt my face go warm. Two could play at that game, but unless I was going to win, I'd rather call it a draw.

Taking mercy on him and myself, I decided to behave. We made small talk until our food arrived. Nothing about our pasts or futures, which was fine by me. This was a first date, not the Inquisition. The conversation was as laid back as The Surf Lodge.

Biting into the lobster roll, my taste buds come alive from the flavor. A little moan escaped.

Sean paused, an oyster halfway to his mouth, his gaze locked on my mouth. "I can't wait until you make that sound for me."

My eyes widened. Sean had the manners of a gentleman and the words of a player. I needed to up my game.

"Consequences, Kelsey. Consequences." Sean slurped an oyster down, which shouldn't have been sexy, but it was. If he wasn't squeamish about the flesh of a shellfish then he'd certainly relish the part of me that was already anticipating the feel of his tongue. Yeah, I really should have worn panties.

The check arrived and I reached for my purse.

"Don't even think about it," Sean said, pulling out his wallet.

I was going to argue but I didn't want to embarrass him. "Thank you, dinner was incredible."

Sean nodded to the seating area on the sand.

"Want to watch the sunset?"

"Love to."

Best first date ever.

Chapter 7

Sean

WE SETTLED ONTO the outdoor lounge chair made for two. Kelsey snuggled up next to me, placing her head on my beating heart, which skipped a beat or two or three. Her body fit perfectly up against mine like we were two pieces of a puzzle.

Off to the side, an employee started a fire in the pit. Other diners had made their way to the sand as well, but Kelsey and I were in our own little world.

We watched the sunset over Fort Pond Bay without talking. Though I wasn't looking into her eyes, in the setting sun it's as if I was.

Though as outgoing as she was beautiful, Kelsey knew how to sit in silence. Most girls would have chatted me to death instead of enjoying the scene being played out before them. Not that I didn't enjoy our dinner conversation, in fact, I couldn't remember a more engaging talk with a member of the opposite sex.

Kelsey didn't talk about boring stuff like clothes or seem to care about the latest celebrity sighting in town. On the flip side, my attempts to learn more about her stalled after learning she was from Georgia. And I still didn't know her last name.

"Do you want another drink?" I asked.

"No thank you. I'm feeling good."

Pleased, I smiled into her hair. Kelsey's scent of vanilla was already as familiar to me as the smells of the beach. I couldn't wait to kiss her and explore her mouth with my tongue. With the crowd growing, this wasn't the place to start something I wouldn't be able to finish.

The sun tucked itself in beyond the horizon. Kelsey shivered. The day had been in the eighties but night temperatures in late June could drop into the upper fifties, and the pretty sundress she wore exposed more skin than it hid. I pulled her closer and rubbed my hands over her arms, trying to generate heat. She shivered again. "I have a jacket in the Jeep, do you want me to get it?"

"I have a better idea."

So did I. "I'm opened to suggestions."

"Why don't we head back to my friend's house and take a walk on the beach?"

I may not know her last name, but she invited me back to her place. Slow down, buddy—she said beach. But it was progress. And there was a strong possibility that 'take a walk on the beach' was code for 'let's do it on the sand.'

I put my arm around her as we walked to the car. The chill of the night caused goose bumps to dance along her skin. I wanted to do more than just warm her. I would make her burn out of control until the air around her felt like a relief.

At my Jeep, I said. "Let me get that jacket for you."

"That's okay." Kelsey pulled out a Penn State sweatshirt from the trunk of her car and put it on.

"Is that where you go to college?"

"Just graduated."

Another piece of information. But right now I didn't care where she was from or who she was. All I needed to know was how her naked body felt against mine. And how many times I could make her come.

"I'll follow you."

"Okay. But try to keep up," she said with a flirty smile.

The ride couldn't go fast enough. When she sped up, I was hoping she felt the same way but maybe she'd changed her mind and was trying to lose me. Or she was driving the Mustang the way it was meant to be driven. The car was made for speed.

And Kelsey's body was made for pleasure.

Finally, she turned off. As I pulled up next to Kelsey's car, I recognized the place.

I got out of the Jeep. "You're friends with Storme Sullivan?"

"Yes. Do you know her?" Kelsey shut the door of her car.

I detected a hint of jealousy in her voice, but she had no reason to be. I didn't run in Storme's circle of friends. "Not really. My buddies and I crashed a party here a couple of years ago."

"She said the girls around here call you Hampton Hottie."

Having the good sense to look sheepish, I cupped the back of my neck and gave it a rub as I said, "I haven't heard that in a long time."

The light off the garage shone on her face and I could tell from her expression she didn't believe me.

"Truth," I said, holding up my hands in surrender. But Kelsey wasn't buying it. What other kind of shit did Storme tell her? "Is that why you didn't call?"

She shook her head. "The forty-eight hour rule."

Stupid rules. "Thought you said you don't play games."

"I don't. I win them."

Her smile was brighter than the spotlight, lighting up more than just the surroundings.

"Am I your trophy?" I teased. But it wouldn't be the first time I'd been a target on a chick's bucket list. And girls say guys are jerks. It used to bother me until I realized there was no harm in it. The chick in question would get what she wanted and so would I.

"I believe that's my line."

I smiled at the truth in her words. "Damn, there goes that fantasy."

Her eyes darkened to amber and she leaned in to whisper, "I'm sure I can fulfill some other ones."

And just like that I'm hard and ready. I loved a girl who knew what she wanted and was not afraid to show it. Especially if what she wanted was me. "Should I grab a blanket?"

"If you need a blanket for one of said fantasies, then yes."

Oh yes, I most certainly did. My brain was racing but my legs were cooler than my head and I didn't act like an unschooled boy. After getting the blanket and my jacket, I held her hand as we followed the pathway to the beach. But I really wanted to hold all of her. A foot away from where the pathway ended, I spotted a private place in the dunes to set up the blanket just in case the night ended the way it was unfolding.

We hit the sand. I dropped the stuff and we tossed off our sandals.

"Race you," she challenged and then took off.

I easily outran her. Not because she wasn't fast but because she wasn't used to running on the sand.

"Damn."

"Not a good loser, are you?"

"My fatal flaw," she admitted.

"Let's try an activity where we both win."

I dipped my head, my lips seeking hers. We connected, our breathing still hampered by the run. A mistake. My heart needed all the oxygen it could get as Kelsey stole what was left away.

Stepping into my embrace, she circled her arms around my neck, and I deepened the kiss, tasting the grapes and vodka she'd drank earlier along with a touch of the sea salt lingering in the air.

I could get drunk simply from kissing her. Simple? There was nothing simple about this girl. I hungered to savor the rest of her body.

Threading one hand from the nape of her delicate neck through her long hair, my other hand cupped the sweet curve of her ass. Our tongues mingled. The roar of my blood replaced the sound of the breaking surf. I felt like I was being dragged out to sea by a rip current. I knew better than to fight it. Hell, I didn't want to fight it.

I'd forgotten how to breathe, only I wasn't desperate for air.

Maybe Kelsey really was a mermaid, breathing for the both of us.

Chapter 8

Kelsey

M Y HEART FLUTTERED like a bird caught in a sudden gust of wind, desperately flapping its wings to regain flight. Sean hadn't lied. Not only was mouth-to-mouth his specialty, he was an expert. Only I wasn't being rescued. Or saved.

I was drowning in an ocean of desire. Some lifeguard he was.

His kiss turned me on and made feel special all at the same time. With his tongue that promised a delicious licking, my body tingled from head to toe.

He nipped at my bottom lip before his mouth left mine. I held back a whimper at the loss. The heavy air around us felt electrified, as if together we were conjuring up a storm. When we touched, when we kissed, sparks darted inside my veins.

"I want you naked, Kelsey."

It wasn't the most romantic thing I'd ever heard, but the way he'd said it, low and tender, resonated through me as if he recited a line of poetry written by Lord Byron.

Perhaps, I should have played hard to get like some girls would have. But romantic or not, I wanted what he wanted. I wasn't going to be coy about it.

"Let's go back to the blanket," I said.

Instead of racing, we held hands. I can't remember the last time I'd held hands with a boy. Junior High? I'd forgotten how sweet it felt. How pure. But my thoughts about Sean were anything but pure.

Sean picked up our stuff and we headed up toward the house. I wondered where he was taking me. About a foot or two up the path he stepped off to the left and onto the dunes. I trailed behind him as he scooted around a batch of sea grass wavering in the breeze.

"How's this?" he asked.

A dip among the dunes protected us from the eyes of the house and the beach. Even with the light from the half moon and the outdoor solar lamp from the pathway, someone would have to know the spot to see us. Still, it was private, secret. Realizing I'd never done the deed under the open skies, I suddenly felt awkward. Was God watching? Was my Dad? Like the roof of a car or a house would matter.

"Good spot," I said, and tried to keep the sudden nerves twisting in my stomach from coming out in my voice.

"Glad you approve." Sean spread the blanket out on the sand then came to stand in front of me. There was just enough light for me to see the desire swimming in his eyes.

The temperature had dropped but I knew I wouldn't be cold for very long. Sean pulled off his shirt and I took off my sweatshirt. I was hesitant to slip off my dress. Why? What was wrong with me? It's not like this was my first time. Or second.

"Don't go all shy on me now. Off," he demanded.

I tugged the dress over my head to reveal my lacy blue bra and the fact that I wore no panties.

Sean dropped to his knees. "Jesus, Kelsey. You should warn a man before revealing such a sexy secret." He looked up at me, his hand over his heart like he was about to swear a solemn oath. "You're more than beautiful."

The compliment made me even more self-conscious. I sensed he was being sincere but one didn't get the moniker Hampton Hottie without being a player. "I bet you say that to all the mermaids." This time my voice shook.

"You're my first." A hint of a smile appeared on his face. "Mermaid, that is."

Just like that he'd eased my worries. "I promise, I'll be gentle," I teased.

Sean ran his hands up my legs and placed a soft kiss at the V at my thighs. I gasped.

Then he looked up at me. A hungry expression had replaced his smile. With complete seriousness he said, "Take that back."

My legs trembled. Wetness slicked in between my legs. "I do. Take it back."

"Lay down with me." Not a demand, but a plea.

It wasn't like I could stand anyway.

Lying on our sides we faced each other on the blanket. Sean caressed my curves so lightly that I couldn't distinguish between his fingertips and the soft ocean breeze until it felt like my whole body was being touched at once, causing me to writhe in pleasure and in agony because I needed more.

I leaned in to kiss him. Soft at first, exactly the way he was touching me. But then Sean threaded his fingers through my hair and kissed me into a wanton frenzy. Pressed against him, my pussy tingled, feeling how big and hard his cock was. I was ready to beg him to fuck me but that would've involved my mouth leaving his.

After maneuvering me onto my back, his lips left mine to trace a path to my breasts. He lightly sucked on my nipple through the lace and then the other. It was erotic. Hot. My breasts wanted out of the confines of the bra. Sean must've felt the same way because with a frustrated yank he set them free. Sucking on my naked nipples, he was greedy now. A moan escaped my mouth. Then another.

Finally, his fingers played with the folds of my pussy.

"Oh, God, Kelsey, you are so wet for me."

"Sean!" I lifted my hips searching for more pressure to bring on the orgasm I could feel building inside me.

"No. I want you to come into my mouth."

His mouth. Yes, his mouth. On my pussy. Now.

The anticipation of his tongue heightened as his lips trailed down from my breasts to my belly and then he is there. His hot breath branded me as his.

"Ah, Kelsey."

This wasn't the time for talk and I pulled his head to where I needed it the most. He understood and licked me. Sucked on me. His hands firmly held my hips in place as he worked my pussy. I clenched the blanket, balling the fabric into my hands. My shouts of his name were lost to the wind. Or at least I hoped so. My body was a bundle of release and desire. I wanted to curl up in a ball. I wanted to ride him hard.

I felt him move away from me. "You taste as sweet as your accent."

Rubbing my legs together, the pleasure continued to hum through me. I'd never experienced anything like it, not even by myself. He knew my body better than I did.

I lifted my head just as he opened a foil packet.

"Let me." I wanted to feel the length and thickness of him in my hands.

"No. Don't move. I love looking at you. Sated. Yet, so ready for more." He rolled on the condom. "So ready for me."

Lying on my back, I could only see a shadow of his cock. I cursed the moon for not being full.

"Open your legs for me, Kelsey."

Not a demand, or a plea, but a prayer.

I answered his so mine could be answered too.

The cool air did nothing to ease the ache between my legs, intensifying the feeling until I thought I would come again.

His cock filled more than my pussy, he was filling every fiber of my being. Like he was a part of me.

"How do you want it, Kelsey?"

I wanted it hard and fast. I wanted it slow and passionate. I wanted it all. Right now. I'd met Sean less than forty-eight hours ago, but my body felt like it had known him forever.

I didn't answer. I couldn't. My breath had caught in my throat.

Sean chose for me as he backed all the way out and then thrusts back in.

"Yes, that!" I cried out.

Each time he pulled out I felt like I was dying and when he pushed back in reborn.

The slow build was torture. It was bliss.

Over and over.

A wave of pleasure crested inside me, higher and higher until I feared, yet still begged for the crash of release.

I was way beyond ready, but I didn't have to tell Sean. He knew my body like we were long lost lovers from another time. Another universe. He quickened the pace to the beat of my pulse. Rapid. Furious.

I might need mouth-to-mouth for real.

Chapter 9

Sean

KELSEY'S NAILS RAKED down my back. The pain felt like a badge of honor.

Hell, it turned me on.

Her pleasure was my pleasure. It was the only way I'd maintained control this long. I wouldn't come until she did. Her sweet moans urged me on. Then her pussy clenched around me, she screamed my name like I was a fucking God, but I was a slave to the very beat of her heart. Raw need hit me like a rogue wave out in the middle of the ocean. And I followed her orgasm with my own.

Coming inside Kelsey was my reward. It was everything.

Our heavy breaths mingled as we both come down from the ride of our lives.

I knew I should say something, but any words

would fall flat compared to how I was feeling. Kelsey wouldn't believe me anyway. I couldn't believe it myself. It was more than her banging body or pretty face. I knew next to nothing about her, yet somehow each touch, each kiss, each sigh felt like a rediscovery. My cock ached to be inside her again. To be home.

I rolled to my back, taking her with me. I held the sides of her face, placing soft kisses on her lips, and hoped my actions relayed what I didn't know how to express with words.

Kelsey shivered against me, snuggling closer for warmth. The cold seeped back into our bodies. Though it was the last thing I wanted, I said, "We should get dressed."

She nodded and pulled away. I immediately regretted my suggestion and nearly stole her clothes to keep her naked and in my arms.

We dressed in silence. She seemed deep in thought and I wondered what was going through her mind. I wished I could read her heart as well I could read her body.

After giving the blanket a shake and tossing it over my shoulder, I reached for her hand. Weaving her fingers with mine, she finally smiled and I knew there'd be a date number two.

Back at the driveway, Kelsey tugged me toward the house. "Do you want to come in for something to drink?"

The only thing I thirsted for were her lips. "I better go. I have drills at the crack of dawn."

"Oh." Kelsey tried to hide her pout.

"Really." I tilted her chin so she had to look me in the eyes. "There's a bonfire at the beach tomorrow night. Come with me?"

"Yes. I'm not nearly done with you, Sean Dempsey."

"Thank God," I said. And when she was done with me, I'd be wrecked. And I didn't care. Pulling her into my arms, I kissed her breath away. "I'll be here by six."

"Wait. Give me your phone."

I fumbled in my pocket and handed it to her.

She typed in her number. I looked at the screen and smiled. Kelsey Mitchell. "So you don't think I'm a serial killer?"

"With the orgasms you give, I couldn't care less if you were on the FBI's most wanted list."

My head swelled along with my cock. I could fall in love with this girl. And that scared the ever-loving shit out of me.

Chapter 10

Kelsey

THE NEXT MORNING the bed won. I had absolutely no desire to take a run on the beach. No desire to do anything but lie here and recover. I ached all over. In some places, the ache was most delicious and in others not.

Splaying a hand across the sheets, I wished Sean were here beside me. Or on top of me. Or underneath me.

A knock sounded. My friends were up before me? Had Hell frozen over? The two didn't wait for an invitation before barging in to jump on the bed.

Leigh grabbed the extra pillow and smacked me on the shoulder. "Wake up!"

"I am up," I grumbled. "What time is it?"

"Ten, sleepy head." Storme opened the curtains. Sunlight poured into the room. "We couldn't wait any longer to hear about your date."

My date. That was a tame way of putting it. Oh sure, it started out so sweet, but ended up oh-so naughty. The thought of it made me smile.

"That good?" asked Leigh.

"Yeah, you look like the cat who just ate the canary—or something else?" said Storme. "Now spill!"

I laughed at my friends who looked at me with expectant eyes. The sun filtering in shined a light on the sad reality that at summer's end there would be no more late night talks or early morning confessions with my girls. We'd go our separate ways; destined to promise to see other soon but ending up merely Facebook friends who liked each other statuses.

Storme would have Philip and the winery, while Leigh worked herself into an early grave as a PR consultant. And I would—I had no idea what. I only knew I had to make the most of this summer.

Knowing it might be my last confession, I relished making them wait as I propped myself up on some pillows. With dramatic flair, I dished about my date with The Hampton Hottie. My friends sighed when I told them about the epic first kiss. My insides went weak from reliving it. It made it real.

"And did it lead to more?" Storme asked like she

already knew the answer.

I answered with a giggle and if the sudden heat in my cheeks were any indication, I think I blushed. Or I was coming down with a cold from swimming in the freezing water, because Kelsey Mitchell did not blush.

"Oh my God! Where?" Leigh hit me with the pillow again.

"On the dunes." But that's all I planned to divulge about the greatest sex of my life. Maybe, because it had felt like it was more than just sex. Had Sean felt it too? Or had the stars, moonlight, and vodka messed with my head?

"It was freezing last night," said Leigh.

"Sean knows how to keep a girl warm," I said with a sly smile.

Storme slapped my thigh through the covers. "You are so bad!"

"Are you going to see him again?" The expression on Leigh's face was hopeful.

I nodded. "He's coming over after work, if that's okay, Storme?"

"Of course it is. Besides we want to check him out for ourselves."

"Okay, but no third degree." My friends should

know by now that I didn't do relationships. Too much drama. "It's a summer fling, not a walk down the aisle."

Leigh shook her head. "Two dates in two days? It must be love."

Yes, that was an anomaly in my love life or more accurately, my lust life. But love? In two days? Ha!

I COMPLETED TWENTY laps in Storme's infinity pool. Wearing little bikinis and large hats, Storme sipped on wine and Leigh nursed a smoothie while they read gossip magazines on the lounge chairs. I swam up to the side and rested one forearm on the lip of the pool. Reaching for the bottle of beer I had left as a reward for my twenty laps, I took a refreshing guzzle.

I pointed my beer at Leigh. "What's up with the smoothie? We're on vacation."

"Hey, I put one of those little umbrellas in it," she defended.

"Doesn't count," I said.

"We'll be drinking at the bonfire. I need to pace myself. And, hello." Leigh waved a magazine with one of the Kardashians on the cover in the air. "It's not like I'm reading War and Peace."

"Only because I hid your Kindle," piped in Storme.

"Excellent idea," I said, smiling as Leigh smacked Storme with the magazine. I took another pull of beer. "What time is it?" I asked.

Storme picked up her phone. "Um, it's 5:50."

It was 5:45 the last tine I asked. Since I wasn't an Olympic swimmer I knew Sean was late and Storme was trying to spare my feelings. I was about to start another twenty laps when Sean let himself in from the gate that led to the beach. "Hello, ladies."

My heart jumped at the sight of him. With his hair tousled in a mess of waves, he looked like he'd come right from work. Had he been anxious to see me? From the lip of the pool, I introduced him to my friends.

"Coming in?" I asked him before they could bombard him with questions. Or flirt with him. What was wrong with me? Storme and Leigh would never do that. But the thought had entered my mind and that was disturbing. Where had this sudden possessiveness come from? With any other guy I wouldn't have cared in the least, always acting so disinterested when they followed me like puppy dogs. Sean could not be classified as a puppy though. He was closer to a man than anyone I had been with.

He cocked an eyebrow. "Oh yeah."

Sean kicked off his sandals and tossed his sun-glasses, along with his wallet to an empty lounge chair then stripped off his shirt. I'd bet a million bucks that Storme and Leigh were salivating like two women in front of an all-you-can-eat dessert bar.

I couldn't be sure because my gaze was locked on his ripped abs. Last night I hadn't gotten a chance to explore the ridges and dips like a game of find your way out of the maze.

Sean performed a perfect cannonball right next to me, dousing my face with water and along with it, my heated thoughts. *Boys.*

"There they are," he said as he swam up to me.

"What?" I hoped he wasn't referring to my breasts.

"Your freckles. I missed them."

Oh. He liked my freckles? I gave him a dubious look.

He touched a few dots on my cheek with the tip of his finger and then some on the other side. "I thought about you all day. I half-expected to see you rise from the sea to taunt me."

Was it his declaration or his touch that made me

all gooey inside? I was feeling too much, too soon and I needed to distance myself from them. From him. From the thought that I could easily fall in love with Sean Dempsey. I blamed Leigh for putting the silly idea in my head.

"Race you." Before I could dart away, his arms shot out, backing me up against the wall of the pool.

"Really? Challenging a lifeguard?"

Darn, I hadn't thought of that. I forget most everything when he looked at me. And the things I did think of revolved around his lips on mine.

"Besides." His hands left the wall and dropped to my hips. "I don't want to race you."

"What do you want to do with me?"

"Truth?"

"Always."

He leaned in and whispered into my ear, "I want to fuck you."

My body responded with an 'oh hell, yeah'. My head though was still clear enough to say, "My friends—"

"Have disappeared."

My friends rocked.

Sean's lips claimed mine in a smoking kiss that told me everything I needed to know. He wanted me just as much as I wanted him. Desperately. The only thing racing was our hearts.

But it was one thing to do it on the dunes by the moonlight and quite another to do it out in the open with the sun still up. It seemed so pornish. And what if Storme and Leigh returned?

Then I remembered the outdoor shower just a few feet away. It was perfect. The roof was opened to the air, three walls made of woven wood slats and a half door, so it gave it the illusion of privacy. Anticipation hummed through my body.

I ended the kiss and took his hand, pulling him to the stairs leading out of the pool. "Come."

"You will, multiple times," said Sean.

We threw the towels over one of the walls. Sean tossed his wallet that he grabbed from the lounge chair onto the bench seat. I was so counting on him to have a condom in one of the folds.

I turned on the faucet, grateful to find there was hot and cold water. Sean ran his hand along my curves, nuzzling my neck as I adjusted the temperature to pleasing warmth. He pulled at the strings of my bikini and just like that I was topless. Was it the idea of getting caught that turned me on or the way Sean massaged my breasts, playing with my nipples in just the right way.

He angled me against his body so the water hit the place between my legs but it was merely a tease and not enough to make me come. Impatient, I took his hand off my breast and slid his hand beneath the waistband of my bikini right to my pussy.

"Ah, Kelsey. That is so fucking hot. You are so fucking hot."

His fingers tapped my clit until I was wet from more than just the water. Then he hooked two fingers and moved them in a pumping motion, rocking my body to a breath-stealing orgasm.

"Sean." I sobbed his name as I came.

I turned in his arms and his lips again claimed mine as the water pulsed down around us. He gave me no chance to recover, backing me up against the wall.

"That's number one."

My body still shook from the release.

Sean dropped to his knees. The water splashed off his chiseled shoulders as he slowly drew down my bikini bottom like he was savoring the act. Placing a small kiss at the v of my thighs, his tongue then moved over my clit in the same rocking motion his fingers had used. The rough siding of the wooden wall dug into my back but I didn't care. The only thing that mattered was Sean's tongue greedily licking my pussy.

My breaths came in short gasps. I didn't know where to put my hands, but they needed to go somewhere before I toppled over. Reaching up, I grabbed the pipe leading to the showerhead not caring if I tore it off. My other hand clutched the back of Sean's head. I felt like I was going to climb up the wall with each little shock of pleasure that grew and grew until my body was on fire.

"Oh, oh, Sean," I cried out. The pleasure was too delicious, too everything. My head hit the wall as I jolted forward and then back, my body shuddering with blessed release.

Sean glided his hands up my legs, then the curve of my hips as he stood. I tasted myself on his lips as he slowly kissed me like it was an art and he a master of it. Like the Leonardo Da Vinci of kissing.

"That's number two."

But when he reached for his wallet, I used all my strength to pull him back and reversed our positions.

I kissed him with abandon, clutching his biceps until I was sure my nails would leave marks. I pulled away and dropped to my knees. "My turn."

The slate tile floor dug into my skin. But I didn't care. I tugged down his shorts, impatient, as he was patient with my bikini bottoms. His cock was beautiful and strong like the rest of him.

My wet pussy warred with my mouth, each wanting possession of his cock. My mouth watered anticipating the taste of him, my pussy dripped from my orgasm.

Mouth to pussy: *I will make him harder and bigger than he's ever been in life and then he'll fuck you with it.*

Pussy to mouth: *Promise?*

Mouth to pussy: *Promise.*

Chapter 11

Sean

WITH NO PRELIMINARY teasing, Kelsey's lips engulfed my cock into the recesses of her hot, wet mouth. A lightning bolt of pleasure shot down my rod at the shock.

Captivated by the erotic sight, I felt the skin of it stretched so tight I feared it would tear. Not that I was about to stop her. She didn't play with it or dabble with it, no; she worked me in and out of her mouth.

It was the cock sucking of my dreams. If it weren't for the shower's cooling mist my body would have combusted into a pile of dust.

"Kelsey, your mouth is so hot."

Were her moans of approval from the size of me filling her mouth? Or did sucking my cock turn her on? Both? Oh hell, yeah. Then she deep-throated me and gagged. Holy. Fuck.

I was a championship swimmer but this chick made my thighs tremble. Tremble! And I loved every fucking second of it.

I was ready to explode but if I did, I'd be rendered useless until later and I'd promised to make her come multiple times and twice was only a couple in my book. I wanted her to burn out of control with me. Reaching for a fist full of her hair, I pulled her mouth off my cock, and then I lifted her up off her knees and up against my hard body. Her soft flesh melded to me, my cock trapped between her legs.

Burying my tongue into her mouth, I kissed her with a passion I had never felt before. The scent of her suntan lotion intoxicated me, as if it was some sort of love spell. She tasted of oranges. And musk, which was probably the flavor of me lingering on her tongue.

I wanted to do more than fuck her. I needed to imprint myself onto her the way she had done to me. To forever change the way she thought or felt about sex. I ended the kiss to begin my mission. "I can't wait to be inside your hot little pussy."

"Hot and wet," she purred.

Holy. Fuck. If there were a world's record for putting on a condom I would have blown it away.

Kelsey now had her back to me, her hands braced against the wood slats. Her sweet ass upturned, ready for me to enter her pussy from behind. It was an invitation that I couldn't refuse. And yet somehow how I did.

Turning her around, I said, "I want to see your face when I make you come."

She tugged on her bottom lip, her eyes alight with fire making me feel as if I were standing on the sun.

Placing one hand on her ass, I gripped a wooden slat for leverage with the other. Kelsey threw her leg around my hip. Wasting no time, I sunk my cock deep into her. Her mouth had showed me no mercy, so I gave her none, pumping in for all that I was worth. Every ounce of myself was giving itself over to her. Her breaths began to come in short gasps and her pussy clutched around me. I leaned back to see her face as she fell apart with me buried inside her.

She was the beauty who had turned me into a beast. And I roared as I came.

Chapter 12
Kelsey

WONDROUS SMELLS LED us into the kitchen. Storme was a great cook, but all I needed was some food as fuel so I could keep up with Sean's god-like stamina.

Sean held my hand and I was a little nervous as we entered the room. I didn't know what to say. I couldn't very well say, 'Sean and I had hot sex in your outdoor shower. And I came multiple times. Three to be exact. Now please feed us.'

Storme broke the ice with a cheeky, "Hope you worked up an appetite."

I looked to Sean who remained bashfully silent. Thank goodness, he wasn't like that in bed. Or rather in the shower. Or on the dunes. An image of us rumpling up the sheets entered my head and my body tingled in anticipation.

"Let's just say I'm starving," I said.

We each took a seat at the farmhouse style kitchen table, which was set up as if HGTV was about to walk in and start filming. Storme played the perfect hostess. The salmon was grilled to perfection and the wine, direct from Storme's family vineyard was divine. I was beginning to relax when they started grilling Sean like he was the piece of salmon on my plate.

"How old are you, Sean?" asked Storme.

"Twenty-two." Sean answered the first question with a good-natured shrug.

"How long have you been a lifeguard?" asked Leigh.

"Since I was sixteen." He raised his wineglass to his lips and took a sip.

"What do you do during the off-season?" asked Storme.

I threw both of my friends the evil eye and made a cutting motion with my knife for them to stop tag teaming my date with questions. Sean and I were nowhere near the stage of talking about the future. I didn't want to know beyond today.

"I travel."

This peaked my interest. Had he been to Europe?

Just like a typical male, he didn't elaborate. My friends were not discouraged from his lack of chattiness.

"Where are you going at the end of this season?"

"Storme," I cautioned, my voice tight, conveying to them both not to be so nosy, even if I was soaking up all this information like a dry sponge that'd been doused with water.

He looked at me. "Actually, I'll be leaving for boot camp down in South Carolina. The Marines."

I blinked. I couldn't have heard that right. The Marines? It couldn't be. The Universe wouldn't be that cruel. I didn't need a man to be rich. Poor, I could handle, but a military man? I couldn't do it. Wouldn't do it. As the oldest, I'd witnessed my Mom suffering through the long absences. Watched her put on a happy face for my sisters and I, even as the constant worry tore her apart. Then, her brave face as she'd accepted the American Flag at my dad's funeral.

Hadn't I already sacrificed enough?

Unable to meet Sean's gaze or utter a single word, I looked away, tears springing to my eyes.

I shouldn't care. What I had with Sean was just a summer romance, a fling. I shouldn't care, but I did. Because I'd already had stupid, crazy feelings for him.

Why couldn't he be a simple lifeguard? But he wasn't. I had to break it off now.

I wished my friends hadn't dug for information. Wished I'd never met Sean. Wished my father were still alive.

Chapter 13

Sean

THE SILENCE DEAFENED my ears. Had they been a part of some anti-war college group? Twenty minutes ago I had been in heaven and now I was in hell as Kelsey's friends interrogated me like they were trying to replace her father.

Holy. Shit.

Had Kelsey's father been a Marine? And had he been killed in action? The tears in her eyes confirmed it. Her friends got up and surrounded her, creating a wall of support, looking at me like I was the enemy.

"You should go," said Leigh.

I shook my head. "I got this."

Storme and Leigh looked at each other over Kelsey's head. Were they using some kind of female telepathy?

"I made her cry, let me dry the tears."

Now they looked at me like I was some sort of alien. Maybe, I was. Truth was, I was scared to death of being alone with Kelsey right now, but I'd feel worse leaving her to deal with emotions that I'd dredged up.

Kelsey nodded and her friends left the kitchen.

Gathering up Kelsey in my arms I said, "I'm so sorry, babe. I didn't know."

"My father—," she sobbed.

Questions burned on my tongue. How had it happened? How long ago? "It's okay, you don't have to say anything if you don't want. I can guess." My tone was soothing, but my insides shredded into pieces. There was nothing I could say to comfort her. Nothing I could do, but hold her.

I reached over for a napkin and handed it to her.

She blew her nose and then blew my mind.

"I can't see you again."

"Whoa." I pulled away but slid my hands along her arms like I was trying to rub some sense back into her. "Nothing has changed between us."

"Everything has. Sean, I'm sorry. I can't do this."

"Do what?"

"Fall for you. You're going to leave and what if— if. I can't even go there."

"Fall for me?" I should have left. But I couldn't.

"Kelsey, tell the truth. What were you planning to do at the end of the summer?"

She blinked. "I…don't know."

I shook my head. "Yes, you do. Like all the other summer girls, you were going to go back home." After breaking my heart, I didn't say. Why was I fighting so hard to keep her close to me? Maybe she was right to break it off now, before one of us got hurt.

"Probably. Home or somewhere else. I haven't planned that far ahead."

"Exactly. Nothing has changed. You're here for the summer, so am I. Let's spend it together."

"And then what, Sean?" She placed her hands on my chest and shoved me away. "You go off to war and get yourself killed?"

Instead of drying her tears, I'd made things much worse. I dragged a hand through my hair. What could I say to the possible truth of what she'd said?

"You should go." Kelsey folded her arms across her waist, looking away from me.

How could she burn for my touch just an hour ago, yet be so cold? *She's still grieving, shithead.* Nothing I could say right now would change her mind.

"This isn't over, Kelsey. It can't be." I placed a tender kiss on her forehead. "I'll see you at the bonfire tonight." It was a statement, not a question.

I KEPT A close eye on Kelsey from the grouping of pickup trucks my buddies had driven onto the beach. The flames from the bonfire shot up into the air casting a glow over her skin. Taking a swig of beer, I tried to quell the urge to go over there and kiss her in front of everyone. To fucking claim her like I was her mate.

She was having fun with her friends, dancing and sipping on beer, oblivious to the fact that every guy on the beach was mesmerized by her moves. It certainly looked like she wasn't second-guessing her decision to break it off with me. Determined to get Kelsey out of my head, I laughed at something my friend said because everyone else was laughing. But my gaze returned to her, drawn back like I was the pathetic moth to her beautiful flame.

Then one of my supposed bros left the group and walked over to the bonfire to put the moves on her. Fucking Blake. My blood boiled as if I were being roasted alive over the bonfire. It was exactly what I would like to do to Blake right now.

Chapter 14

Kelsey

ALCOHOL BUZZED IN my blood. My heart thumped to the beat of the loud music as I danced with Storme and Leigh. The bonfire's flames were hot and the beer cold. The scent of smoke mingled with the salt-kissed air.

The stars sprinkled across the night sky. A perfect summer night, except Sean wasn't there to share it with me. Smiling at me. Snuggling on the blanket by the fire. Waiting for the perfect time to sneak a kiss. To sneak off to do more.

Since Sean had left the house I had done an admirable job of convincing my friends that I was okay. In fact, I should forget architecture and run off to Hollywood to become an actress that's how good I was. So good that I had fooled myself into believing I wanted nothing to do with Sean. Until now.

Why had I completely lost it on him? Once he'd left Storme's kitchen, he'd probably realized I was more trouble than I was worth. That's why he wasn't here. He was avoiding me and I couldn't blame him. I'd taken a simple summer romance that was all of three days old and blown it into a star-crossed lovers tragic romance.

I was about to reach into my pocket for my phone to text an apology when I felt a tap on my shoulder. Thinking it was Sean I swirled around, ready to throw myself into his arms.

"Remember me?"

"Oh." It was the lifeguard who asked me to play the victim yesterday. He was super cute, but he wasn't the one I wanted to be with. I bit my lip to keep the disappointment from my voice. "Yeah, you're Sean's friend." Hopefully, he'd take the hint and leave me alone.

"Which makes me your friend." He tried to slide his arm around my waist, but I slipped from his grasp right into Sean's arms.

Where I belonged. At least for the summer, I did.

"Beat it, Blake."

"Sorry, bro. I thought—

"You thought wrong."

I nuzzled Sean's neck, breathing in his masculine scent of sea spray and leather. What was wrong with me? I'd never felt like this about a guy before.

Glad to see his friend get lost, I backed away and gave Sean a little shake. "What took you so long? I've been here for hours."

"Missed me?"

By the cocky look on his face he already knew the answer. I wanted to kiss him until he transformed into a longing, hungering, mess. But first we needed to set things straight. "We need to talk."

We walked to the shoreline, away from the crowd and the music. He didn't take my hand. Why? And why after such a short time was I missing it? I needed some reassurance, so I risked taking his. A sigh of relief escaped me when he squeezed my hand.

At the water's edge, he turned to me. Taking my other hand, our gazes met and my mouth went dry with the words I couldn't form. In the moonlight his blue eyes appeared ethereal, like they were calling to me. This place was magical, that was the only way to explain the rush of tingles in my blood and the reason why I would risk my heart.

"Sean, I'm sorry I freaked out on you."

"Don't be. I understand, I do. I'm being selfish. I

want you."

"I want you too. I want to spend the summer with you, but I can't give you more than that." Even if I fell in love with him, even if my heart was ruined forever when I had to say good-bye, it would be worth it because I'd put myself out there without regret.

"That's all I'm asking for, Kelsey." He raised my hand to his lips and kissed it. "One perfect summer. One perfect memory. I swear I won't ask for more."

All these mushy girly feelings were sweeping me away. I had no idea how to process them. Was I really falling in love? Was he? I didn't want to break his heart any more than I wanted him to break mine. "One more thing. No talk of the future. No talk of the past."

He nodded. "So it sounds like you just want sex?"

"Lots of sex."

"You drive a hard bargain." With a crooked smile, the cocky look was back in full force.

I snorted. "I—"

Farther down the beach we heard shouting.

Sean turned and scanned the water before looking to the sand where a couple of people were dipping their toes into the water. Turning back to me, he released a breath. "Sorry, it's an occupational hazard.

What were you going to say?"

"Nothing." I'd forgotten. I smiled, liking his dedication to the job. "Let's find a non-water view, so all of your attention is focused on me."

"I know just the spot," he said.

Sean certainly knew mine.

Chapter 15
Kelsey

ONE WEEK LATER, Storme fussed in the dressing room of the fancy bridal boutique, while Leigh and I lounged on plump pink chairs and sipped champagne. Sipped? The reality of my friend getting married had finally sunk in and I downed a flute like it was a shot of Tequila.

Storme floated out of the dressing room and onto the platform. After performing a spin, she stood in front of us. My hand covered my open mouth. Coifed and bejeweled, she looked like she had just stepped off the last page of fairytale.

"You look gorgeous, Storme." I finally said. "Prettier than any *Modern Bride* magazine cover."

"I'm not going to be able to hold it together at this wedding." Leigh blotted the corner of each eye. "You're perfect." It looked liked she was not going to wait until the wedding to cry.

I couldn't blame her. Storme was the picture perfect bride that every girl dreamed of being one day.

Even me. Eventually. Like a decade from now. But so taken with the moment, I envisioned my own wedding.

The dress? Strapless, a-line silhouette, with a jewel encrusted waistline.

The venue? Barnyard Chic.

The flowers? Magnolias and white roses.

Music? Country Rock.

The groom? Sean.

Whoa! Slow down, girl.

But the foolish thought made me smile. So, shouldn't Storme be smiling at her reflection? Was she having second thoughts? "Uh, oh. That is not a happy face." I said. "What is going on?"

"I-I think I'm having bridal jitters. Totally normal, right?"

Tears sprung to Storme's eyes as the saleswoman waltzed in with a cheery smile and a rambling sales pitch for fun honeymoon items. I leapt off my chair like it was on fire. "Not now, please. We have a crisis."

Following my lead, Leigh jumped to her feet.

"Yes, no interruptions, please and more champagne."

The saleswoman, probably used to meltdowns like this, disappeared without a word as the bride-to-be sat between her bridesmaids. The tulle of the dress spread over our laps in a fluffy cloud. Storme knocked back the glass of champagne Leigh had handed her and then we both listened as she spilled out her heart.

Holy crap! Her and Philip only had sex one time!

I downed another glass of champagne, trying to wrap my head around it.

Marriage without sex? They'd be doomed from the moment they vowed 'I do'.

And there was more. Storme had kissed another man. The hot biker dude I'd seen hitting on her at the bar a couple of nights ago.

Leigh suggested that Storme tell Philip about the kiss and her doubts.

I nodded like I'd agreed but I didn't, not about the kiss. "Your hormones blew up and you couldn't help yourself. Having no sex will do that to a person."

"I suck." Storme looked ready to fall apart. "I feel like an adulteress."

The miserable look on my friend's face tore at my gut. "You're not married yet so you can't be an adulteress," I blurted. Maybe the alcohol had gone to my head, but I suggested the unthinkable. "But this is a sign you have to figure out if Philip is really the man you should marry. Can you really spend the rest of your life with a man without any physical connection?"

I wouldn't blurt out that I thought Philip was Mr. Wrong, with or without hot biker dude in the picture. If she did marry Philip, then I'd be the bad one. The one who'd tried to tear them apart.

Leigh leaned forward. "Tell us the truth. Do you really want to marry Philip? Or do you feel like you have no choice?"

Storme seemed torn about her decision. I knew I'd made the right decision not to say anything more. The turbo extra large vibrator I ordered as a gag gift for the bachelorette party wouldn't be a gag at all, more like a necessity.

Storme and Leigh went back and forth while I remained silent.

"Call Philip, tell him the truth about the kiss, and your doubts. Then try to come to a decision together," advised Leigh.

Storme played with the material of her dress. "I guess that would be the right thing to do."

I exchanged a wary glance with Leigh and nodded. "We'll back your decision. Whatever it is. We'll celebrate with you if you get married, and help you escape if you want to be a runaway bride."

Stormed drained the glass of champagne. "Thanks guys. I'm better now. You're right. I'm going to call him when I get home. Try to figure it out together. I just don't want a cheap physical attraction to distract me from my real future."

Even though she said she was better, the look on her face said she wasn't. I knew I had to lighten the mood so I giggled and said, "Hey, I happen to adore cheap physical attractions."

Storme seemed relieved by the opportunity to take the focus off of her as she said, "That's because you're hooked up with the hottest lifeguard in the Hamptons. How is Sean?"

With Sean, the attraction went beyond the physical. Sex had always been about attaining the almighty O, but truthfully until Sean I'd never experienced it. Not that I didn't enjoy sex before, I did, but Sean made me feel with my very being. With my heart. I needed to take a large step back from that thought. I reminded myself we were all about the sex. "Sean is good. Very, very good."

"Slut," Leigh teased.

I raised a brow. "What about you? Care to tell us what's been going on between you and Nick?" I'd seen this Nick guy and her getting cozy at the bonfire earlier in the week. The faint blush on Leigh's cheeks told me nothing had happened yet.

Too bad, I thought. It seemed like I'd be the only one having fun this summer. Yep, that vibrator was going to be a *huge* hit at the bachelorette party.

Chapter 16

Sean

THE LATE JULY temperatures set records but it was nothing compared to the way Kelsey scorched up my nights. By day I worked the stand at Main Beach. Sometimes Kelsey and her friends would stop by for a couple of hours. But today she was solo, frolicking in the water in front of me.

Yep, frolicking. That was the only way to describe it.

The late-morning sun shone off her golden tanned skin. The white crochet bikini she wore was designed to torture mere mortal men like me. I had no idea how the material held up her ample breasts. The perfectly tied bows at the side of the bottoms beckoned my fingers to tug at its strings to unravel the prize beneath.

Though the white flags were up, the greedy Atlantic Ocean waves would wash her suit out to sea. Which is probably why she was teasing the water with only her toes and teasing me with the rest of her body, along with every damn man on the beach including Blake, who shared the stand with me today.

I looked away, twirling my whistle out of habit and concentrated on the group of forty-something ladies navigating the waves while their children dove in ahead of them. Yet my gaze kept returning to Kelsey, tracking her movement along the shore. Never had any girl tempted me from my duties as a lifeguard. Never.

"Man, she's a danger to public safety," said Blake.

A hot blade of jealousy slashed through my gut. Enough.

I blew my whistle, capturing her and everyone else's attention. I waved her over. With the sun on my back, Kelsey crooked a hand over her sunglasses as she approached the stand.

"Am I in trouble?" Her tone, naughty and flirty, left no doubt to her preferred form of punishment.

"Yeah, for indecent exposure."

"Wait until I get wet."

"Damn, Kelsey."

Blake whistled and not with his standard issue

lifeguard whistle.

"Whoops. I didn't mean it THAT way."

"Sure you didn't. Go home and take a nap. I want you rested for later."

"Sean, that would be sexy if you didn't currently look like a Smurf."

Touching my nose, I'd forgotten about the blue zinc oxide I'd smeared on this and every morning so I wouldn't end up with skin cancer in a couple of years. "You'll pay for that."

"What? I think it's adorable. And it matches your eyes."

"Seriously, Kelsey, go home and stop torturing me."

She stuck out her tongue before spinning on her heel to sashay back to her towel.

Yep, sashayed.

"Oh, how he mighty have fallen," said Blake.

"Yeah, what was your first clue?"

"Dude, you're Mr. Lifeguard, and you looked away from the water for two seconds."

If only it were a mere two seconds. "That's why I asked her to leave. She's my Kryptonite. I think I love her, man."

"Here." Kelsey held up a brown paper bag.

Crap. Had she heard any of that? We'd agreed to keep the relationship fun. If she suspected that my feelings ran deeper than just sex would she back off?

"Hello." She waved the bag. "I made you lunch."

"Oh." I reached down and opened the bag to peek in.

"And I bought you an energy drink, because YOU'RE going to need it later."

I welcomed the challenge. Closing the bag, I said, "Thanks, babe."

"Welcome." She turned to go.

"Hey, Kelsey."

She stopped, placing a hand on her hip. "What?"

I pointed the whistle at her bikini. "Wear that under your dress tonight."

"Wear the blue stuff on your nose," she quipped back.

Laughing, I turned my gaze to the water. Guarding lives was a hell of a lot easier than guarding my heart.

"I'd say she's got it bad for you, too," said Blake.

I twirled the whistle like a cowboy with his gun, pretending I didn't care if what Blake said was true, but I still asked nonchalantly, "You think?"

"Dude, she made it clear to all the other chicks on

the beach that you are hers."

Heart, body, and soul.

Could it be that Kelsey's feelings ran deeper, too? Is that why she made her way to my beach on most days when she could have sunbathed by Storme's house? Why she'd made me lunch today? And why she couldn't get enough of me at night?

My break wasn't for another hour but I was suddenly hungry. Opening the bag, I unwrapped the foil, relieved to find none of that health food crap that she liked to eat. Hearty roast beef with all the fixings on a sub roll. I'd save the energy drink for later, because I knew Kelsey wasn't lying when she'd said I'd need it.

"Are you going to share that sandwich?"

"Not a chance." The sandwich was mine. And so was Kelsey. At least until the end of the summer.

LATER THAT NIGHT, I found myself soaking in my first bubble bath since I was a little boy, only instead of a rubber duck as a companion, I had a hot playmate sitting across from me. Vanilla scented candles surrounded us, and music played softly in the background. The swell of Kelsey's breasts peeked above the bubbles. I was damn tempted to pull the drain cap so I could see her whole body, slippery and wet, wearing only bubbles.

Though we'd been barely able to keep our hands off of each other, I still wanted more, but Kelsey seemed far away. Maybe, I wiped her out, which would be a first. But something told me it wasn't that.

"Hey, what's the matter?"

"It's nothing." Kelsey took a handful of bubbles and formed her beautiful mouth into a perfect O and blew. I smiled but her return smile was strained.

True to our agreement neither of us talked about the future. But somewhere along the way it became more than just sex for me. Way more than a summer romance. I wanted to help her with whatever was going on in that beautiful mind of hers. Hell, I wanted to take care of her. Solve every problem. Fix anything that was broken. But I didn't have the right. In a couple of months, I'd be thousands of miles from her. Even if the thought of her living her life without me hurt, I'd take the pain to ease hers.

"Bullshit." I scooped up some bubbles with a finger and dotted her nose. "Talk to me.

Chapter 17
Kelsey

TALK TO HIM? How could I? He was going off to war and I was trying to decide between the comforts of home in Georgia or going to Europe to extend my studies and my fun. Except without my friends—without Sean, the prospect of Europe held no appeal. Nothing did. I wanted this summer to last forever—for us to last forever. How foolish to think I could keep my growing love for Sean in a box and like Pandora, if I opened the lid there would be no going back.

What I couldn't express verbally, I did with my touch. Our gazes silently communicated what we felt. What we had moved beyond sex. Or maybe my brain was weaving this into a tragic Shakespearean play when in reality it was a comedy with the joke being on me if Sean didn't feel the same way. If that was the case, then ignorance was truly bliss.

"I can't. The rules of our relationship—"

"Rules are made to be broken. Especially if you're the one who made them."

Sean's intense gaze held mine. He seemed to be holding his breath. Had he been waiting for a signal that I wanted more? One part of me did, the other part—the one that was winning, didn't want to end up like my mother. Worse than alone, grieving for the love of your life. I looked away. "You agreed to them."

"I would have agreed to anything if it meant seeing you again."

My gaze darted back to his. The candlelight wavered in his blue eyes making them appear to be same color and texture as a swimming pool lit up at night. I could surely drown in them and not care if I was rescued. I didn't know if it was the languid feeling from soaking in the bubbles, the candlelight, the beer, or the fact that I trusted him as a lover and as a friend, but I decided at that moment to share more than just my body with Sean.

"Okay then. I don't know what to do after the summer is over."

"Any ideas?"

"Well, option one, I go home. Get a job." Then find a nice but boring guy and train him to give me orgasms like you.

"Option two?"

"Go to Europe, get my MBA in architecture engineering." Then study like mad and try to forget you.

"Architecture? Engineering? How come I didn't know that?"

"Don't look so surprised!" I smacked his leg, which cause a ripple of water to splash up over the side of the tub. "I'm smart."

"Of that I have no doubt. It's a tough field and you're a female."

"I don't know which is worse, you thinking I'm dumb or that you're a sexist." I took a sip of beer.

"To be clear, I never thought you were dumb. And I'm not sexist just a realist."

"Which is why you probably think Europe is a dumb idea."

"No, you should go before you settle down."

Did he mean settle down with a job or a man? Did he even care that after the summer I might find someone else? Would Sean be a 'girl in every city' type of soldier? Or would he be a one-woman man and find a girl who could withstand the lonely nights.

Either scenario drove me crazy with jealousy.

"It's a pipe dream."

"What's stopping you?"

"Money." He knew I wasn't a rich girl like Storme. "There are no volleyball scholarships for MBA programs."

"Sell the car."

"I can't sell my Dad's car! It's the only thing I have of him."

Sean downed the rest of his beer and placed it on the windowsill. "You've told me about your mom and your sisters, but you've never told me about him."

Only because it was too painful to talk about, but so was not talking about him. Remembering him. "It took my Dad ten years to restore the Mustang. When he was home on leave, he'd be out in the garage tinkering with it. I'd bring him some sweet tea and we'd talk for hours. As I got older he'd let me help."

"A daddy's girl."

"Yeah. And a tomboy," I admitted. Sean reached for my hand. I took a shuddering breath trying to contain the wetness in my eyes. "He loved that car. My mom went into labor when they were looking at it. In fact, he wanted to call me Shelby. My mom refused, so they compromised on the name Kelsey and he purchased the broken down Shelby Mustang."

Sean laughed. So did I.

"Anyway, I can't sell his dream."

"That's just it Kelsey, it was *his* dream. Maybe he left the car to you so if he wasn't around, it would give you the money to follow your dream."

I blinked. That sounded exactly like my dad. Why hadn't I thought of it? But Sean had. I could sell the car, and not only pursue my dream, but also help my younger sisters. It felt right, like my dad had been waiting for me to come to that realization.

"You know my Dad would've liked you."

Sean chuckled and shook his head. "No, he wouldn't."

"Why do you say that?" Sean was an all around good guy and a future Marine.

"Uh…because I'm having sex with his daughter."

"Oh yeah, he'd have killed you." I went silent realizing what I'd said.

"Kelsey, it's okay to talk about him."

I smiled and nodded. It felt good. For the first time since his death I was able to remember my father with laughter. "Thanks. Now can I ask you something?"

Sean reached over to the cooler for another beer.

"Sure." He popped the top and took a swig.

"Why the military?"

He nearly choked as he swallowed. I could tell he was measuring his words before he said them. "The simple answer is that I was raised to serve at an early age. My church. My school. My community. And now my country, like all the other Dempsey males."

I nodded, like I understood his decision to enter the armed forces, as if it would help me to understand my father's call to duty. But it didn't. Not that I wasn't proud of my father. I was. So very, very proud. But proud didn't get me my father at my college graduation. It wouldn't get me my dream of having my father walk me down the aisle at my wedding. *Proud wouldn't get me Sean.*

"Why architecture engineering? And what's the difference?"

Relieved to be talking about something else, I delved into my answer. "It's more than the design of a building, it's about the materials, and the surround-ings of the site. My focus is on creating new sustainable communities."

"Ambitious."

"I wasn't raised to be a Southern Belle. Being a Marine's daughter, I know how to change a flat, know the basic self-defense moves, *in addition* to baking a mean pecan pie."

"Pie. I like pie." His hand drifted up my soapy thigh.

He was so cocky and sure of himself. Of me. I gripped his hand to stop his progress. "Say pretty please." I gave his wrist a little twist to show off one of those self-defense moves.

The light in his eyes turned to blue fire. "May, I please touch your pretty pussy?" he asked in a rough whisper.

I melted at the low desperate timber of his voice. I let go surrendering to him and to the fact that I had no self-defenses when it came to Sean, whether it was my body or my heart. None at all.

He moved forward to position himself between my legs. Water sloshed over the sides of the tub.

"Um, Sean, we're going to the flood the floor."

"Not a problem." Sean flipped the toggle of the drain to the down position and the water started to recede, the sound of it in stark contrast to the romantic music in the background. "Just you, me and the bubbles, babe."

Chapter 18

Sean

MY DEPARTURE LOOMED over us like the tropical storm bearing down on the East Coast. The day had been sunny and hot with no indication of the upcoming storm, but the ocean knew, as it always did. The rough surf kept the swimmers out of the water but not away from the beach, making it a busy day of whistle blowing.

Night had fallen, but the temperatures hadn't. Even though Storme had given us free reign of the house, Kelsey and I gravitated to our favorite spot. In the dunes, under the cover of darkness, we pretended that time stood still.

A gust of wind ruffled the blanket as we spread it out on the sand. We laughed as we pinned it down with our bodies. Our gazes met when we rolled to face each other. The laughter faded. I think she was about to cry. Or maybe I was.

In a week, I'd be gone. All summer I had tried to convince myself I could walk away unscathed, but I was a fool. Kelsey had stolen my heart, along with pieces of my soul, and that was the painful truth. Thing was, I didn't want any of it back. What use would I have for a heart?

"Make love to me, Sean."

Make love? Though she only whispered it, the words echoed inside me as if she'd shouted it at the top of her lungs, down into the emptiness of my being. It was the closest we'd come to saying it, though I had admitted it to myself countless times. I never had the balls to tell her. What good would it do? She had made up her mind and I wouldn't be the cause of any more pain for her.

I undressed her like I was unwrapping a precious gift. Every day we had left would be. Kelsey returned the favor, shedding my shirt and shorts with a purposeful slowness. And then we were skin to skin. Softness and hardness.

Running her fingers down my six-pack, her touch seared as much as it soothed. I wanted to throw her onto her back and ravage her but I remembered her plea to make love.

I swept my hand possessively along the curves of her body. For now, she belonged to me. In my heart, she always would.

I kissed her sweet lips, imprinting the feel and the taste of them in my soul. Gathering each moment into a memory that would last me in the years to come without her.

Her body pressed against mine, searching for more. I would give her everything. Give her all of me. I didn't need daylight to map out each freckle with a lick of my tongue. I knew every inch of her.

Just when I was getting to the best part, licking Kelsey's red velvet pussy to a wet nirvana, she sat up and pushed me onto my back. "I can't wait. I need you inside me now."

So. Fucking. Hot.

When Kelsey took the lead I was in for it good. And I loved every second of it. But this time, after rolling on the condom, Kelsey slid down my rigid cock oh-so slow. Taking me inch by inch, until her hot pussy consumed every inch of me.

She massaged her breasts as she moved her shapely hips back and forth in a rocking motion that rocked my world then turned it upside down.

So. Fucking. Hot.

Any minute I was going to come without her. I placed my thumb on her clit, applying a gentle pressure.

Her sweet moans echoed in the night. "Oh, Sean."

Moonbeams spilled across her body and the ethereal creature that was pleasuring herself with my cock enthralled me. I feared that in time this would become only a dream. It wouldn't even be a memory, just a myth I'd created. That it never really happened. Because how could something so beautiful have ever happened to me? To any man?

Did it matter? Whether memories or dreams, her erotic moans would haunt me for the rest of my days.

Chapter 19

Kelsey

MY BODY HAD come to need him in the same way I needed air. Not just the sex or his handsome face, but also the masculine feel of him, the smell of sun on his skin, and the sound of his voice whispering my name. Everything. *How do I love thee? Let me count the ways.* Oh, Elizabeth Barrett Browning, you had it so right.

His thumb pressed against my clit, scorching my already heated skin. His cock, big and hard, filled me with pleasure, but I didn't want either of us to come, not yet. I wasn't ready to lose the connection of our bodies joined as one.

I didn't know how I would let Sean go. I only knew that it would happen. And there was nothing I could do about it. Emotions swirled inside my head. Joy. Sadness. Ecstasy. Pain. Loss. Love. My movements became desperate. Hot tears stung my cheeks.

"It's okay, babe," whispered Sean as he gently rolled me onto my back, his cock never leaving my body as he did so. "I know."

His thrusts were deep and true. Reaching a part of me I never knew existed. A slow steady rush of bliss coursed through my veins, until it had nowhere to go and then pooled and built up inside me.

"Kelsey, I can feel you. That's it, babe. Make me come with you."

Then I was there. A breath caught in my throat. I couldn't inhale or exhale as I crested with each wave of intense pleasure and yes, pain. Sean's name ripped from my throat out into the night. Over and over I sobbed his name, as I completely lost myself to him.

The release cleansed me of all the conflicting emotions and all that was left behind was the love that I couldn't express.

Sean lifted his head away from my neck. His breath, hot and heavy mingled with mine. His skin slicked with sweat blended with mine. We were a beautiful mess.

He stretched out beside me. In the sweet hush of the aftermath of our loving-making, I wanted to stay there forever looking up at the stars with his hand stroking the curve of my hip. I don't know how long we stayed like that. A minute. An hour? A lifetime? The stillness of the night ended as the wind kicked up.

"The weather is turning, we better get inside." Sean's voice was filled with regret.

So much for forever. Fearing if I spoke I'd blurt out that I loved him, I put my clothes back on in silence, remembering how he'd slipped off each piece with a reverence reserved for holy ceremonies.

Sean had gone mute too. Did he think I was a lunatic female for crying during sex? As the summer waned, my love for Sean had not, it had only grown with each passing day and night. I had become unhinged at the thought of him leaving me, of him going to war.

Clothed, I turned to him. He'd been watching me. Maybe it's the moonlight shining in his eyes, but I saw love there, though he'd never told me. I didn't want him to. *Yes, you do.*

He reached out and stroked my cheek with his thumb. Had a tear left a track of wetness? Leaning into the caress, I asked, "Will you stay with me tonight?"

Sean palmed my cheek. "Yes, and every night until I—"

Leave. The unspoken word hung between us like a dark shadow. Sean kissed me with a tenderness that shattered my heart as if he'd taken a sledgehammer to it instead. How could he kiss me like that and leave me?

Without warning, he froze, and then pulled away. Sean tilted his head, his brows furrowed.

"What's wrong?"

"Shhh!"

I didn't take offense to his sharp, annoyed shushing. He'd heard something. Was someone coming down the path? Had someone heard us making love? Straining my ears, I listened too. A faraway cry of help carried on the wind.

Sean leapt up. "Bring our phones." He bolted to the walkway and took the turn that led to the beach.

Startled, it took me a moment to spring into action. I grabbed my purse along with the blanket and raced after him. Ahead of me, Sean had angled off on the sand and ran to the water about twenty feet from Storme's part of the beach. Breathless, I joined him at the shoreline. Sean had already stripped his shirt off and had his hands up to his forehead in a V shape to scan the ocean.

"Where is she?"

I didn't think he was even talking to me, but I asked, "Who?" All I saw were huge thunderous waves, crashing to the shore.

"There." Sean pointed.

I barely made out the slight form in water. To my untrained eye it could have been a piece of driftwood.

"Call 911." Sean instructed. "Stay on shore."

He didn't wait for a response, diving into the treacherous waves with no hesitation or concern for his own safety. My heart clutched in fear for the girl and for Sean. My hands shook as I pulled my phone out of my purse and pushed the buttons for 9-1-1, while I tried to track Sean's progress at the same time. I didn't want to lose sight of him or I might just lose myself.

"911, what is your emergency?"

In a rush I explained the situation, thinking the faster I spoke, the faster they'd get here.

"Miss, please slow down."

Slow down? It's an emergency! I took a deep breath. I spoke again, this time slower, so my accent wasn't hindering the dispatcher's understanding. Somehow, I remembered Storme's address.

"Help is on the way. Stay on the line, Miss. Do

not hang up."

If only someone could throw Sean a line. I wished I could do more. I wished I were a mermaid. But my swimming skills were no match for the turbulent water. I would only hinder Sean's efforts and I needed to stay on shore in case...in case...please, God help them both.

Chapter 20

Sean

THE HAMPTONS HAD seen its fair share of hurricanes and tropical storms. I had made plenty of ocean rescues before, but never at night, never without the backup of another lifeguard and never without any safety equipment.

Huge barrel waves rolled in without mercy. Past the breakers, the ocean was turbulent and angry, like it was looking for a sacrifice. Between the incoming storm, the high tide and the full moon, everything was working against me. Except, I had Kelsey on shore to call 911 and direct any rescue crews to where I was.

Breaking the surface, I didn't see the girl. Fuck! She was there just seconds ago. Panic ricocheted inside my chest. *Where is she?*

I took deep breath in an effort to calm myself.

Then two feet in front of me, right where she was supposed to be, the little girl popped up and bobbed in the water like a rag doll.

I jerked out my hand and pulled her to me before she was lost to me again. "I got you," I said as I placed her in a classic lifeguard's hold. She whimpered but her breathing was shallow. Too shallow.

I guessed her age to be about ten years old. What the hell was she doing out here dressed in a one-piece bathing suit like it was a sunny day at the beach? "I won't let go."

"Promise," she mumbled.

"I promise," I swore as I looked back to the beach.

There was no easy way in. No path of least resistance. I had to get us back to shore now. I couldn't wait for a break in the waves or for help to arrive. The weather was deteriorating fast. By the way the water swirled to the left of us, I suspected a rip current. I doubled checked my hold on the girl, and then kicked to the right with all the strength I possessed. A huge wave took us under, violently spinning us until I had no idea which way is up. My lungs burned for air. But I wouldn't let her go. I'd promised.

If the sea drowned us, it would be with my arms clutched around her. She would not die alone. Her little body went limp. A bad sign. Had I crushed her? Had water filled her lungs? There was nothing I could do but hold on. My back hit the bottom with a thud and I almost lost my grip from the force of the blow. Sand and shells scraped my body as I was dragged along and then we were tumbling again. Defenseless against the raw power of the ocean, it was only by some miracle the wave released us and spit us out onto the shore like a rocket.

Adrenaline pumped through my body, giving me the strength to carry the non-responsive figure in my arms to the dry sand. "She's not breathing."

Still on the phone, a tearful Kelsey updated 911.

I placed the cold body on the blanket that Kelsey had laid out. Putting the heel of my right hand on the small fragile chest, I began compressions.

"Yes, Sean's beginning CPR now."

Thirty compressions. Two breaths.

"They're five minutes out." Kelsey powered up the flashlight app on her phone to provide me with light. Smart chick.

Thirty compressions. Two breaths.

I repeated the procedure again and again, until it stopped being a procedure and became a prayer.

Thirty compressions. Two breaths.

Fuck! She wasn't responding. *Please God.* The phone's light cast an eerie glow over the girl. With all my training, I didn't panic. Not yet. But I couldn't lose this little one. No way.

Thirty compressions. Two breaths.

"Come on baby, breathe," Kelsey half yelled, half cried.

Thirty compressions. Two breaths.

Then the sweetest music to a lifeguard's ears sounded. A cough, followed by a gurgling sputter, then water spewed out of the girl's mouth.

"It's okay." I rolled her to her side and gently patted her back, but I didn't know if I'd said the words for the little girl or for myself. "It's okay."

Chapter 21

Kelsey

S EAN HAD SAVED a little girl's life. Pulled her from the ocean like a man possessed and performed CPR as if his own life depended on it. The unbearable weight pressing against my chest lifted. It was like now that she could breathe, I could too.

After the girl spit out the last of the water, I wrapped the sides of the blanket around her shivering body and held her close to me.

"I want my Mommy," she croaked.

"I know you do, sweetie." Where were her parents? How did she leave her house and get down to the beach without them knowing it? She shivered again, despite the muggy air. "What's your name?"

"B..b..bonnie."

"Bonnie? That's such a pretty name," I soothed.

Over the head of the girl, my tearful gaze met

Sean's. His face was a mask of relief and exhaustion. The need to protect was so engrained in him that he didn't realize he was a hero. But I did.

Isn't that the type of man I should want?

Isn't that the type of man that any woman would be lucky to have?

Why was I fighting my feelings? Denying them? I was such a hypocrite to tell Storme and Leigh to follow their hearts when I'd run in the opposite direction from mine. Away from Sean. He wasn't anything like any of the college boys I'd dated. Not even close. Sean was a man. A good man. Everything a man should be.

And I'd almost lost him.

In that moment, I finally understood my mother's sacrifice. And why she said she'd do it all over again. Even after losing my father.

And why I would do the same for Sean. For myself. For the two of us.

I love him. That's what it came down to. It was so simple. There was no choice to be made. There never had been. I love him and I didn't want to live a life without him. I'd take each goodbye knowing each homecoming would be worth it all.

I may be a daddy's girl but I was more like my

mother than I'd thought. I could be strong like her. I now realized her strength was more powerful than any army's. Still, to reveal one's heart took a different kind of courage.

I had to tell him I wanted forever. "Sean, I—"

I heard the sirens before I saw the lights. Sean grabbed my phone and waved it in the air as a beacon for the ambulance that was racing down the beach to our location.

The EMTs jumped out and I released a reluctant Bonnie to them. Sean gave them a rundown as they immediately assessed the girl's condition. Several ocean rescue trucks and a police SUV arrived on the scene seconds later. I stayed in the background as Sean repeated the information to someone who looked in charge. I recognized some of the other rescuers and Blake, who tossed a blanket over Sean's shoulders. The respect and admiration they all had for him was clear from the way they hung on his every word.

The EMTs were preparing the girl for transport to the hospital for further evaluation when a man and woman raced down the walkway from the house next to Storme's, shouting. "Bonnie! Bonnie!"

I directed them over to the ambulance just as they

were about to shut the doors. "Bonnie. Oh, my God. What happened?"

"I just wanted to go swimming." The girl's big blue eyes filled with enough tears to flood the Hamptons.

As the girl's parents hugged and scolded their daughter at the same time, I turned to Sean who watched the scene with a smile. If Sean and I hadn't met, if we hadn't made love on the beach tonight, if Sean hadn't been skilled, if he hadn't been brave, if the ocean had been any worse, they would have lost their child. So many ifs had to line up to save Bonnie. Life offered no guarantees. The only thing you could do was embrace life in the here and now.

Done with the authorities, Sean walked over to me. My heart cracked opened from the love filling into it. There was nothing left to do but share that love with him.

"He saved me." The girl pointed to Sean.

The mother ran over and hugged him tight. "Thank you. Thank you."

Sean nodded to me. "You should thank Kelsey, too."

"Me? But I didn't do anything." I didn't risk my life or perform CPR.

But the mother hugged me anyway. "Thank you, for saving our little Bonnie." Then the mother got into the ambulance for the ride to the hospital.

The father shook his head. "She was mad at us for not letting her in the water today. I don't know how she snuck out." The father was still reeling from almost losing his daughter.

Sean poked his head into the ambulance. "Hey kiddo, no more swimming without a lifeguard present."

"I won't."

"Promise?"

Bonnie smiled. "Promise." She bestowed a kiss on his check. "Thank you."

He leaned back out and her father shook Sean's hand. "I don't know how I'll ever repay you."

Sean touched his cheek where the little girl had kissed it. "Bonnie just did."

Happy tears pooled in my eyes. I looked down to the sand, ashamed of how stupid I was with Sean after playing his practice victim when, fooling around, I had said the exact same words. The wind kicked up and a light rain began to mist as the ambulance drove off. Sean shared his blanket with me, slipping a corner around my shoulder then circling an arm around my waist. His body was still damp.

"We need to get you out of those wet shorts," I said.

"I just bet you do."

Looking around at the others gathered around us, my eyes widened with horror. "Sean! That's not what I meant!"

But Sean and everyone else in hearing distance laughed. "I know you didn't, babe." He kissed the top of my head.

I felt the heat of a blush in my cheeks, but the joke seemed to lighten the mood so I laughed, too.

We walked back to the house huddled under the blanket to ward off the wind and rain in silence. My brain had enough inner chatter to drown out the sounds of the encroaching storm.

I knew I would have to be the one to break the rules. Sean would never break his vow and ask for more than what I'd offered at the beginning of the summer. He was too noble to do otherwise. Besides they were my rules to break.

I hoped he wanted our summer romance to be endless and forever like I did. Because I didn't think I was strong enough to survive his rejection.

Chapter 22

Sean

KELSEY LED ME back to the house and demanded I take a hot shower – without her. Was it punishment for the joke I'd made on the beach about her needing to get me out of my shorts? If so, it was a cruel punishment. The pulsing water jets washed the adrenaline I'd been feeding off of down the drain and I was crashing hard.

My muscles ached and before I fell asleep standing up, I got out and dried off. Kelsey had left the bedroom so I slipped on a robe she had left out on the bed. I'm guessing it belonged to Storme's dad. Or perhaps rich people who owned houses like this kept robes handy for their guests. The bed alone looked like it belonged in a magazine.

The bed. My body wanted to sprawl out on top and sleep until morning, but not without Kelsey to warm me.

I walked down the staircase with the intention of hauling her back upstairs. She was in the kitchen wearing cute knickers pajama bottoms and a t-shirt with the word Georgia Peach emblazoned below a decal of the fruit. My mouth watered and not for the soup that wafted in the air.

Outside the storm raged. Wind, sand, and rain pelted the windows.

"Where are Storme and Leigh?"

Kelsey looked up. "Leigh had to run home for a family emergency and Storme is out enjoying one last night of freedom before her parents get back."

I nodded. "Where are my clothes?"

"You won't be needing them anytime soon."

I arched an eyebrow.

"Meaning, that as soon as I get some soup into you, you'll be sleeping." She led me to the couch. She tucked a throw blanket around me and puffed a pillow behind my back. "I'll be right back."

She wasn't kidding. A second later, she handed me a bowl of chicken soup. I'd rather have a shot of whiskey, but after taking a few sips I started to feel better.

Kelsey continued to fuss over me and I let her because after what had happened I knew she needed to. And I admit, I liked it. I had never seen this nurturing side of Kelsey before. Yeah, she was a hugger and liked to spoon but taking care of me outside of the bedroom? That was new.

And seeing how she'd mothered Bonnie had got me thinking about having children with Kelsey one day. I had no right going there, even in my head.

She had almost lost me to the sea tonight. *And you never told her that you love her.*

Even though I couldn't ask for us to stay together, she had the right to hear the words. And I couldn't go away without saying them. I tried to put the soup mug down, but she grabbed it and did it for me. "I love you, Kelsey Mitchell."

The widest smile appeared on her face. "I love you too, Sean."

She loved me? My heart thundered. Great, she loved me, but I could never go against my vow and ask for more than this summer. Even if she wanted to stay together, it wouldn't be fair to ask her to wait for me. "I'm sorry."

Her brow furrowed. "What for?"

"Because it will make saying goodbye harder."

Kelsey straddled my legs. The Georgia Peach right

in my line of sight. With a finger, she tilted my head up so my gaze met hers. "But that's just the thing, Sean. I can't say goodbye to you. At least not the forever kind of goodbye."

Did I drown for real and this was some afterlife joke?

Pushing at my shoulders, she said, "Did you hear me, Sean? I love you. And we are not breaking up when you leave."

Before I agreed, hell, before I begged to stay together, I said, "I can't ask that of you." Not after what she'd gone through with her dad.

"Well, I'm not asking you to ask me, Sean Dempsey! I'm telling you how it's going to be." The amber fire in her eyes warmed me more than the hot shower or the soup ever could.

"Hell, you are a Marine's daughter, through and through." I hadn't realized how strong she was until that moment.

"Damn straight." Kelsey tugged on the lapels of the robe. "And I will make the best Marine girlfriend ever."

Girlfriend? She was more than that to me. I wanted more than that. Since Kelsey had thrown out the rulebook, I decided to risk it all. "You'd make the best

Marine's *bride* ever."

Her eyes widened, the light shining in them enough to burn through the storm raging outside. "Are you proposing to me?"

I tucked a strand of her hair behind her ear. "Kelsey, will you marry me?"

She covered her mouth with both hands. Fuck, was she holding in a no?

Then she released her hands. "Yes!" She placed a big kiss on my mouth. "Yes!" Then another kiss. "Yes!"

Between the kisses and the way she rocked her hips on my lap, my cock was not registering the romance of the moment at all.

She pulled away. "Wait, you're not going to try to talk me out of going to Europe, are you?"

"Wouldn't dream of it. Just don't go falling for some sweet talking Euro douche bag."

"Not a chance. I like my men the way I like my cars."

"How's that?"

"All-American and all muscle." She rocked her hips again. "And I do believe I'm being saluted by some American muscle right now."

"Hey, I thought I was supposed to get some

sleep," I teased.

"Your cock is not cooperating. It's wide awake."

"Maybe, it needs you to *hum* it a lullaby."

A half smile tilted on her face. "Why Sean, how almost poetic of you."

"You mouth is poetry in motion." I threaded my fingers through her hair, urging her head down so her lips met mine in a scorching kiss that matched the storm's fury outside and my wild raging heart within.

Kelsey pulled away. "When?" she asked in a breathless whisper.

"When what?" My brain was currently in my pants.

She nudged my shoulder. "The wedding? When do you want to get married?"

"Tomorrow?"

"Men." She rolled her eyes. "I may not need a fancy wedding but I do need more than a day. My family has to travel, I need a dress—"

"Shh." I placed my finger to the lips I so desperately wanted back on mine. "Just as long as you're officially mine before I leave."

She smiled, her eyes full of warmth and desire. She pushed my finger away. "And after Storme's wedding. I don't want to take away from her day."

"Great." I nodded, ready to agree to most anything. "Now can we get back to kissing?"

Kelsey answered in the best way possible. Without a word.

The End

Thank you for taking the time to read Summer Dreaming. If you enjoyed it, please consider telling your friends or posting a short review. Word of mouth is an author's best friend and much appreciated.

And don't forget to check out the rest of the Hot in the Hamptons series with Summer Temptation by Wendy S. Marcus and Summer Sins by Jennifer Probst!

Keep the burn going with the next 2 books in the Hot in the Hamptons series…

Summer Temptation
By Wendy S. Marcus

Meet Leigh DeGray...

After graduating college with honors and landing the job of my dreams in New York City, I'm off to The Hamptons to spend the summer with my two best friends. My life seems perfect, right? It's not. Because I have a secret that may make the future I'd planned so carefully completely fall apart. A hot summer romance is the absolute last thing I'm looking for. Until I meet a man who tempts me like no other and shows me a hot summer romance is exactly what I need.

Meet Nick Kenzy...

After two years of working my ass off as a Wall Street analyst, I'm out of a job, with no warning, no thank you, and no severance. Am I angry? You're damn right I am. So when I head to the Hamptons for the weekend to spend time with my granddad, I plan to regroup and relax before I return to the city to hit the job search hard. I don't need any distractions. Until I meet Leigh. And suddenly, a summer temptation makes me question everything...

And

Summer Sins
by Jennifer Probst

Summer fun before my wedding…

I have one goal this summer. Hang with my besties for some much needed sun, sand, and relaxation while I put the final touches on my idyllic wedding. I didn't count on meeting a smart-mouthed, bad boy biker whose gaze burns hotter than a beach bonfire. I never planned to lose myself, body and soul, and question my entire future. Now, I have to make a choice that's tearing me apart, and could shatter the lives of the two men I love…

Turns into summer sins….

I have one goal this summer. CHILL. Do nothing. Nada. I need simple before I have to head into Manhattan to take on a high powered position on Wall Street. I didn't count on a dark haired, inky-eyed spitfire who'd spin my world upside down, or make me burn for things I never thought I wanted. I vowed to make her my summer fling, but had no idea she was claimed by another. And now that she possessed not only my body but my soul, the stakes are too high for me to lose her…

About the Author

Liz Matis is a mild mannered accountant by day and romance author by night. Married 29 years she believes in happily-ever-after!

Fun Fact: Liz read her first romance at the age of fifteen and soon after wrote her first romances starring her friends and their latest crushes!

Fun Fact 2: Liz kept an inspiration board for Summer Dreaming on Pinterest. Check it out here: www.pinterest.com/lizmatis

Keep in touch with Liz at:

Website:

www.lizmatis.com

Blog:

www.taoofliz.blogspot.com

Email:

elizabethmatis@gmail.com

Twitter:

@LizMatis

Facebook:

Liz Matis Fan Page

Goodreads:

www.goodreads.com/author/show/5289185.Liz_Matis

To sign up for my newsletter please contact Liz at:
elizabethmatis@gmail.com

Also by Liz Matis

Fantasy Football Romance Series Box Set

From bestselling author, Liz Matis, comes the box set of the popular Fantasy Football Romance series! Includes the award-winning and #1 bestseller in Sports Fiction, Playing For Keeps, along with Going For It – also a #1 bestseller in Sports Fiction, Huddle Up, and The Quarterback Sneak, which also reached #1. The series has over 600 four and five stars reviews on Goodreads!

Or start the series with Playing For Keeps.

Journalist Samantha Jameson always wanted to be one of the boys, but Ryan Terell won't let her join the club. Fresh from the battlegrounds of Iraq, reporting on a bunch of overgrown boys playing pro football is just the change of scenery she needs. If trying to be taken seriously in the world of sports writing wasn't hard enough, Ryan, her college crush, is only making it harder. As a tight-end for the team she's covering, he is strictly off limits.

Ryan Terell is a playmaker on and off the field, but when Samantha uncovers his moves, he throws out the playbook. Just as he claims his sweetest victory, Samantha's investigation into a steroid scandal involving his team forces him to call a time-out to their off the record trysts. But then a life threatening injury on the field will force them both to decide just how far they'll go to win the game.

Winner of the NECRWA First Kiss Contest.

Other books by Liz...

Love By Design by Liz Matis

Design Intervention starts the second season with its own surprise makeover. Interior designer Victoria Bryce must break in her temporary co-host, Aussie Russ Rowland.

Sparks fly on camera as they argue over paint colors and measurement mishaps leading to passions igniting behind the scenes. But when their pasts collide with the present will the foundation they built withstand the final reveal? An HGTV meets Sex and the City romp!

Real Men Don't Drink Appletinis by Liz Matis

Hollywood's handsomest men surround celebrity agent Ava Gardner but none are as intriguing as larger-than-life Grady O'Flynn. The Navy SEAL is on an unsanctioned mission when they end up starring in their own romantic comedy.

Will they continue to sizzle when Grady has to report back to duty? In this sexy novelette by Liz Matis, two lovers have two weeks to find out.

Coming Soon:

Fall 2015
My Zombie BFF

CPSIA information can be obtained
at www.ICGtesting.com
Printed in the USA
FFOW03n2111210817
39114FF